Tempting the Texas Tycoon

SARA ORWIG

First published in Great Britain 2011
Large Print edition 2011
Harlequin Mills & Boon Limited,
Eton House, 18-24 Paradise Road,
Richmond, Surrey TW9 1SR

ISBN: 978 0 263 21671 4

Harlequin Mills & Boon policy is to use papers that
are natural, renewable and recyclable products and
made from wood grown in sustainable forests. The
logging and manufacturing process conform to the legal
environmental regulations of the country of origin.

Printed and bound in Great Britain
by CPI Antony Rowe, Chippenham, Wiltshire

SARA ORWIG

lives in Oklahoma. She has a patient husband who will take her on research trips anywhere from big cities to old forts. She is an avid collector of Western history books. With a master's degree in English, Sara has written historical romance, mainstream fiction and contemporary romance. Books are beloved treasures that take Sara to magical worlds, and she loves both reading and writing them.

With many thanks to Krista Stroever,
who made this book possible,
and to Maureen Walters, who has done
so much. Thanks, too, to Shana Smith
and Katherine Arathoon.
Always, love to my family.

Prologue

"Here's to you, Dad," Noah Brand said, raising his glass of Dom Pérignon in a toast.

"Happy birthday." Jeff lifted his glass, too, a mirror image of his twin with thick black hair, gray eyes, a firm jaw. Both were three inches over six feet tall and their builds were similar. Jeff's distinct personality showed in his preference for Western suits and boots.

"Thank you, boys. We'll go join the others, but I wanted a private moment while the two of you are here." Knox sipped his drink, holding their attention in typical fashion.

Worry fluttered in Noah because his father's

health, although not terrible, wasn't as good as it once was. A slight breeze came through open French doors. It was the fourth of March and already Dallas had signs of spring.

"You're thirty-four years old now," Knox continued, looking directly at Noah, who suddenly felt as if this talk were directed to him more than Jeff. "I see no deep female relationship happening for either of you," Knox said, and Noah relaxed, knowing his father was just going to try to meddle in their lives. Once again Jeff would tune out the rest of the conversation.

"You're in the prime of life. My biological clock is ticking as well as your mother's. We would like to see both of you married and more settled."

"Dad, damn," Jeff said, and Knox waved his hand.

"Hear me out. I know I can't dictate when either of you will marry. I know you both like women and have had close relationships, but they never get too deep and never, ever last. Neither of you even asked to bring a woman to the party tonight."

"This is a family deal," Jeff said, and Noah wondered if Jeff would go all his life butting heads with their dad. There were better ways of managing people. And much faster ones.

"All I want to do is make you both at least think about the possibilities. Tell you what, if either of you marries within a year from to-night, I will give you a present of five million dollars."

Noah couldn't resist a smile, and Jeff laughed aloud, shaking his head as he stood.

"Sit, Jeff. I'm not finished. As a bonus, the first one of you to marry will get an additional two million."

Jeff's smile vanished. "So you're pitting us against each other again," he said in disgust while Noah held back any comment.

"It's just an additional incentive. Two million will not make or break either one of you. You've both done well for yourselves."

"Well, thanks, Dad," Jeff said, the cynical note clear in his tone of voice as he stood. "I'm going back to the party." In long strides he was out of the room, letting the door swing shut behind him. Noah and Knox looked at each other.

"You expect me to get that extra two million," Noah said.

"I know you're competitive, as well as cooperative, and I know Jeff is a rebel."

Noah swirled the drink he held and stood. "Dad, I'd like to keep you and Mom happy, but marriage isn't even on my horizon."

"In many ways marriage is a small part of life, Noah. Our leather business is where you'll spend your time. You have enough wealth to do as you please and keep a woman happy. You'll find children are a blessing—they're important. Find a woman from your friends, someone you can get along with, and start a family. You'll never regret it."

"I'll think about that," Noah said. "Your guests may be missing you by now, Dad. Let's rejoin the party."

Knox strode across the room and walked out with Noah, joining the crowd in the great room where they held parties. Noah saw Jeff standing alone and strolled over to him.

"Once again he's played us against each other," Jeff repeated. "Well, bro, this is one time you have my permission to win. I'll step back out of the way."

Noah laughed. "Frankly, I was going to let you win this time. All seven mil. I'm not in the marriage market, and as good as it seems to have seven mil tossed in my lap for nothing, I don't see marriage happening. You know I've always said I don't want to marry until I'm in my forties. I don't want to take Dad's advice and just find someone to marry because I can afford to keep her happy, and I'll be busy with work."

Jeff had been taking a drink and almost choked with his laughter. "Son of a gun! He's got it all planned for you. What a prospect! Of course, that's what he and Mom have and they're both happy. Mom can shop and travel to her heart's content. We grew up with nannies—that isn't what I want in my life and I am not getting married to please Dad or for some bonus. He always has to try to control our lives. I don't know how you stand working with him constantly. Makes me love my ranch twice as much."

"Dad and I are so busy with our leather business, acquiring more stores, upgrading products, adding lines. We hardly see each other." Noah set down his champagne flute. "We better mingle with the company. Let's have lunch soon, Jeff."

"Sure, if you can tear yourself away from Brand Enterprises. I'll be here three or four more days for a cattle auction. How about Monday noonish?" Jeff suggested as Noah agreed and walked away, his thoughts turning to those men in the crowd it would be advantageous to talk to for business. He wasn't marrying soon. At present there wasn't even a woman in his life.

One

Emilio Cabrera smiled broadly as he greeted his granddaughter Monday morning and received a hug from her. Faith Cabrera felt a rush of love for him, wishing she could do more to help him.

"Good morning," she said.

"Ah, how did I ever get such a beautiful granddaughter?"

She smiled. "Thanks, Granddad. Could it be you're a little prejudiced?" She smoothed a wayward tendril of blond hair back in place.

"So what's happening in our world this morning?" Emilio asked.

Faith waved a piece of paper she had received from their receptionist-secretary, Angie Nelson. "For one thing we've had another call from someone with Brand Enterprises. I'm not taking any more calls from those people."

Emilio nodded. "They can't get it through their collective heads that I won't sell our family business. They think I'm old and need to give it up."

"That's not it, Granddad," she said, always hating to hear him talk about getting older. "I've always been told that they've been after this company since it started. I have never known if that's what started the feud between the two families or if the feud came first, causing them to try to buy us out."

"The feud goes so far back, even I can't answer your question completely. What I do know is that my grandfather and my father both fought the Brands. There were buildings and trucks damaged. We have some bullet holes in the back of this building from Brands shoot-ing at our family. No one was ever sent to their grave, but it was bad. Trucks run off the road, all sorts of things. The violence ended with my father and there's never been any that involved my generation. Now it's bitter feelings. Of course, the Cabreras blame the Brands. Just as the Brands said they were here first and blame the Cabreras. Don't you worry over it. I don't mind telling them no again."

"I intend to see that you don't have to deal with them. I'll handle the Brands. Or rather, avoid the Brands. They've wasted enough of our time."

"When I walked in, I saw you poring over the books. How did we do last month?"

"I haven't gotten it tallied," she said, trying to avoid getting specific until she checked thoroughly, but their sales were still slipping.

"You don't have it tallied, or you don't want to worry your grandfather?" he asked with a twinkle in his dark eyes. Even though he would be seventy-nine this year, he still had some dark hair sprinkled with the gray curls that covered his head. He was a master craftsman and once again, she regretted that there weren't any family members left to carry on the craft.

"I know you can handle the truth about Cabrera Custom Leathers, and we're still in the black, I'm sure."

Nodding, he stepped away. "I don't know what I'd do without you, but I wish you hadn't given up your own job running that department store."

"We've been over that, Granddad," she said with a smile.

He left the room and she straightened her shoulders.

As she ran her hand along the antique mahogany desk, she touched scratches from years of wear. In a corner of her office an ancient saddle was mounted on a wood stand, her great-great-grandfather's saddle that he had made and then used for years. This office was part of her grandfather. He was the most important person in her life and she intended to protect him from the Brands.

She returned to her desk to get back to work until the next person knocked at her open office door and she looked up to see their tall, sandy-haired receptionist. "Come in, Angie," she said, wondering what was causing Angie's panicked expression.

"Faith, I stepped out to pick up our mail and I saw a limo parked out front. A tall man in a suit was getting out."

"A limo in this old industrial part of town? Even rarer than the suit."

"That's what I thought," Angie said. "It's not exactly jeans and overalls."

"Chances are the Brand company again," Faith snapped while her mind raced. "Thanks, Angie. I'm slipping out the back. I have errands anyway. I don't want to talk to another Brand employee, not even Noah Brand himself," she said, still surprised that a week earlier, after two calls from a vice president, the COO of Brand Enterprises had called her. She hadn't taken his call.

"Stall him briefly while I leave. I'll have my cell phone. You can honestly tell him that I'm not here. They quit long ago trying to talk to Granddad, so they won't ask for him." As she grabbed her purse and a book, she rushed for the door. "Thanks a million."

Stepping into the shaded alley, Faith let the door swing shut behind her. When a shadow moved, she spun around. With a gasp she looked into thickly lashed, dancing gray eyes that appeared filled with amusement. Slight creases bracketed his well-shaped mouth. Startled, she knew she was facing Noah Brand.

"Miss Cabrera," he said in a deep voice, "I'm Noah Brand." He offered his hand.

"Mr. Brand—" she said, hating to shake hands with him, but unable to avoid the polite gesture. The minute his warm hand closed firmly around hers, a tingle raced from his touch. She was held as much by his grip as his steady gaze that drove all thoughts of business out of mind.

"Sorry if you're late for an appointment," he said. "You seem in a big rush."

"I am. I—"

"I've tried to contact you, but of course, I had no idea how beautiful the youngest Cabrera in this business is. Had I known, I would have been here sooner."

"Mr. Brand—" she tried again, feeling her face flush.

"It's Noah, Faith," he said, both names rolling off his tongue, stirring a flash of warmth in her. She made an effort to break the unwavering stare as she removed her hand from his.

"With families that go back for generations—since the Cabreras first settled here—I'm surprised we haven't crossed paths before now. The Brands go as far back as the Cabreras do."

"And the Brands have been trying to buy out their competition since the beginning. Your family has always been after mine. Unsuccessfully, I might add," she said, causing a faint smile.

"Are you saying your family is stubborn?" he teased.

"No, I'm saying we like what we do and aren't worried about our competitors."

To her chagrin, he chuckled.

"As I understand it, you're handling the business side for your grandfather. I'd like to talk to you about the future of your company and present an offer we have. It never hurts to listen."

Exasperated, she faced him, even though it was difficult to keep her mind on business. The man was drop-dead handsome and she could feel an unwanted, fiery chemistry sending her pulse racing. She fought an urge to smooth her hair. "Of course," she said without thinking, and realized she had just succumbed to his mesmerizing spell. "Just not at this moment," she added hastily. What had gotten into her to be so dazzled by the man's mere appearance?

"How about over dinner tonight?" he asked, moving a step closer. She could faintly detect an enticing aftershave. "You might be pleasantly surprised by what I have to say. It would benefit your grandfather tremendously."

He was smooth, she'd give him that. He'd hit on the one reason she might possibly listen to his plans. "In these circumstances, isn't a dinner invitation an unorthodox way to present a business deal?" she asked. "Your family has been after my family's leather business for generations and it's always been no. That hasn't changed."

"You don't even know what I'm going to say.

Don't you at least want to know what we have in mind?"

"I can well guess. I doubt if it's changed much from the last time you talked Granddad into seeing you," she said.

"It might be worth more to you now," he said. "And your granddad has worked a long time. He's bound to have considered retirement."

"Granddad is far from wanting to retire. He's doing what he loves," she said, letting her animosity show with a harsher tone. "Thank you for the dinner invitation," she said, inching toward her car, which was parked in her space at the back door. "I really can't discuss business now. I have another engagement," she said stiffly, knowing she had no such thing, but she wasn't going out with Noah Brand to listen to his annoying sales pitch.

After she had unlocked her car, Noah's hand stretched out to open the door for her. Glancing up, she met a dazzling smile that made her knees weak.

"When my grandfather is ready to talk, I'll call you, Mr.—"

"No," he said, shaking his head. "I told you, call me Noah, Faith."

For the second time, when he said her name, it stirred a tingling inside. "It was nice to meet you," she said, knowing that statement was the biggest stretch of all. It had been unnerving and disconcerting to encounter so much sexy charisma in the COO of Brand Enterprises. Sliding into her car, she closed the door.

Noah stood watching her, looking relaxed and in command, with one hand in a pocket of his navy suit trousers. His demeanor didn't resemble that of a man who had just been rebuffed. Far from it. He looked as if he already owned her grandfather's business. She knew down to her toes she hadn't seen the last of Noah Brand.

Annoyed with herself for even looking at him, she put her car in gear. He stepped out of the way and she drove off as the back of her neck prickled. She glanced in her rearview mirror to see him still standing outside her door.

Feeling ruffled and unnerved, she drove to her condo near the residential area where her grandfather had lived since he was a young man. Trees had leafed out and early spring flowers bloomed in beds. How happy she'd been to leave her condo for work earlier only to return now to work at home because she wanted to avoid another encounter with a Brand.

Lively gray eyes came to mind and she blinked, shaking her head. She had no intention of spending time with him. The vast Brand leather business wanted to swallow up her family's small boot and saddle business. Why Brand was so persistent she didn't know, because Cabrera was only a blip on the Brand radar. But she could guess why. They could match or exceed Brand for craftsmanship, as well as fine leathers, too. A pair of Cabrera boots had sold for as much as $75,000. They were worn by presidents, royalty, stars, celebrities of all types, as well as by cowboys, oilmen and various other people. She had seen the Brand names on the customer list. The Cabrera name meant the pinnacle of craftsmanship and luxurious leather.

Her granddad didn't want to sell out. Nor

had her father or her great-grandfather or even her great-great grandfather. She thought about Noah's dinner invitation. What a shame—she would have accepted in a flash if he hadn't been a Brand. As it was, Noah Brand was the last person on this whole earth she cared to spend an evening with.

Noah watched her drive away and smiled, rubbing the back of his neck and wishing she had agreed to go out. No one had mentioned that Faith Cabrera was a stunning woman. He knew she was single, twenty-eight years old, refusing to sell because her grandfather didn't want to relinquish the business.

As he headed to his car, Noah wondered if his vice president of marketing had already gone back to the office in the limo. It had been a ploy that had worked to a degree. He'd flushed her out and talked briefly. Patience and time, he reminded himself. He'd get Cabrera Leathers, just as he had gotten other businesses he'd gone after.

Thinking about blue eyes and full, rosy lips,

he drove back to the plain vanilla office building in a complex of three tall buildings that housed the current Brand Enterprises headquarters.

Faith Cabrera was a beauty—that attraction between them had been sizzling. He could tell she felt it, too. Even though she had attempted to be polite, her hostility showed. He hadn't met a woman who couldn't be won over and he didn't expect Faith to be any different from the others. Only a degree more challenging.

Entering his office that occupied the top floor of the twenty-story red-brick building, he sat at his desk to go over the morning calls. After a light tap at his open door, his assistant, Holly Lombard, entered his office.

All business, from her conservative hunter-green suit to her thick auburn hair in a bun on top of her head, she was efficient, and about as driven as he was. Unlike him, Holly was very engaged. As she sat across from him and set folders in her lap, she smiled.

"Tell me you got to talk to one of the Cabreras."

"I did," he said. "And good morning to you.

How are you and the fiancé? When I saw you last Friday, you said you thought he was going to set a date."

She smiled. "Yes, as a matter of fact we did. Doug and I are getting married in December."

"Congratulations," Noah said, studying her briefly. "That's a long way off."

She shrugged. "We have busy schedules and he has some business projects coming up, so there we are. Now, tell me about the Cabreras. Which one did you talk to? Let me guess—the granddaughter."

"Shrewd girl. It was Faith Cabrera. I struck out, but I've met her and I'll try again. I'll see her eventually," he said, hoping it would be soon.

"She was successful where she worked before. She moved up to chief buyer in the huge retail chain she was with. She's probably pretty sharp."

"Maybe I'll be able to hire her. I want the grandfather's methods, craftsmanship and expertise. I could use her, as well."

Holly smiled. "I know how much you like a contest." She slid a folder across his desk. "I have some purchasing agreements I need you to sign."

"Let me have them," he said, taking a stack of papers from her. "Get me an appointment to talk to our marketing vice president. I want to know how he's coming on the deal to buy the leather company in El Paso."

"Will do," she said, waiting while he signed the purchase orders and handed them back to her. She left the room and closed the door behind her quietly.

As he worked the rest of the morning, Noah's thoughts kept returning to Faith. How to approach her again?

Promptly at noon he left the office to meet his brother for lunch. Jeff slid out of a booth and waved. Noah told the hostess he had spotted his brother.

She smiled. "He had me fooled, Mr. Brand. I thought it was you."

"I won't ever be here in boots and jeans. That's the way to tell. My brother's a cowboy," Noah said, accustomed to the remark he'd been hearing all his life. He was amused when people thought they were alike. Jeff was far more laid-back, devil-may-care.

Noah shook hands with Jeff before he sat in a booth across from him. "We could have eaten at my office and had all this brought in."

"Glad we didn't. I don't want to run into Dad. Found you a wife yet?" Jeff asked with a wide grin.

Noah laughed and shook his head. "Dad can never stop trying to get what he wants. In business and in our lives."

"Amen to that one. He spent an hour the other night trying to get me to come back into the business."

"I'd be glad to have you," Noah said, at the same time feeling the prickle of rivalry that he always felt when he and Jeff became involved in the same thing.

"Thanks, but no thanks. Which falls on deaf ears with Dad. I don't know how you stand the corporate life and keeping Dad happy all the time, but you always did that."

"Not altogether. I'm failing at the one thing he wants badly."

"The old grab for the Cabrera business. Dad hates to give up. Even though he failed at it, too." Jeff paused while a waiter came to take their orders and bring ice water. As soon as they were alone, Noah returned to what he had been telling Jeff. "It hasn't changed now that the granddaughter has stepped in. She won't even talk to me."

As Jeff set down his water, he laughed. "A woman who won't talk to you. Is she married?"

"No, she's not married, and she's gorgeous."

"And won't talk to you?" Jeff said with an arch of one dark eyebrow. "Well, you're slipping, bro. Want me to don a suit and step in for you and get an appointment?"

"Don't flatter yourself," Noah said, accustomed to their good-natured teasing. "I'll get that appointment sooner or later." They paused again while their waiter brought grilled chicken sandwiches and small garden salads. They ate in silence for a few minutes until Jeff put down his fork, sipped his water and looked at Noah.

"Why the big grin?" Noah asked, wondering what devilment Jeff had in mind.

"Because I remembered a way you can have an evening with Faith Cabrera if you really want it badly. Of course, if you're not up to it and the lady *is* gorgeous, I might step in for you."

"We haven't done that since we were kids. Get back to how I can have an evening with her."

"I have a friend who knows her. You remember Millie Waters. According to her, Faith Cabrera is one of the women who has agreed to participate in a bachelorette auction this weekend. It'll be held Friday night."

"A bachelorette auction," Noah mulled, seeing his opportunity. "She doesn't strike me as the type, but it's free publicity, and their business is antiquated."

"It may be antiquated, but they still make the best boots in the business. Traitor that I am, I own eight pairs of them."

"Damn, you're a walking advertisement. You should stick to Brand boots out of loyalty."

"You sound more like Dad by the day. Consider it competitive research. That old man Cabrera knows how to make a perfect boot. Brand Enterprises probably gives them cold chills. Big corporation with mass marketing." Jeff put down his sandwich. "As a matter of fact, I may have stuck that ticket in my wallet. I bought one from Millie. She had five tickets she had volunteered to sell."

"I can buy one from her."

"No need," Jeff replied, fishing in his pocket. He tossed a small red ticket on the table. "Be my guest. Should be an interesting evening. If you win the bid, Faith Cabrera will have to be pleasant to you."

"Thanks," Noah said, picking up the ticket. He raised an eyebrow. "Let me pay you for this. This is a high-dollar deal—the ticket costs a fortune."

"Forget it." Jeff dismissed the offer. "Cancer research is a good cause. Spend a small fortune to buy the lady and then the rest is up to you," Jeff said, grinning wickedly and Noah smiled in return.

"I will do just that."

"You better stop licking your chops. She may be a cool customer." Jeff added.

"We'll see. Thanks for the ticket."

"I'm looking for a new truck while I'm here, and I'm meeting Uncle Shelby for dinner tonight."

"He spent about twenty minutes at Dad's party and then left."

"Things between them will never change," Jeff said. "As much as our uncle loves Europe, he's never forgiven Dad for putting him in charge of European sales and getting him out of headquarters."

"Uncle Shelby has a chip on his shoulder," Noah said, seeing the cool look in Jeff's eyes.

"We don't need to fight their fight," Jeff replied. "I better get going. Thanks for the lunch."

"Thanks for the ticket to the auction. This is going to be a real pleasure."

"Enjoy yourself," Jeff said, laughing as he left.

After lunch Noah drove back to his office,

wishing the week had already passed. He would be at that auction and he *would* get his evening with Faith and when it was over, he might be on the way to acquiring the Cabrera boot business. A sensational deal for him. Even better, he hoped he could not only charm the lady, but also seduce her. Big crystal-blue eyes, lush breasts and gorgeous blond hair. He looked forward to melting the ice from that gaze.

Two

With butterflies in her stomach, Faith smoothed her tan leather skirt. She wore a short tan leather jacket, a matching silk shirt. Critically eyeing her skirt, which ended above her knees, she twisted to view herself from several angles. "I hope this outfit shows off my boots," she said, glancing down at her elegant Cabrera boots. She adjusted the hand-tooled Cabrera belt.

"No one can miss your boots. You look super," Angie commented.

"Thanks, Angie," Faith said, studying herself in the mirror. "We're all set."

"I've checked on the participants wearing

Cabrera products. Our part is done," Angie assured her, stepping back. "And I hope you get a ravishing hottie bidder who will show you a good time."

"My friend Hank said he would bid and my cousin's friend Rafe Hunter will be here to start the bidding if Hank doesn't," Faith replied, her thoughts on her blond hair, which swung freely across her shoulders. "Would you please check my hair in back, Angie?"

"It's super."

"Thanks for your help tonight."

"Sure. Good luck. Have a blast."

"Thanks," Faith said, wrinkling her nose and wishing the whole weekend was over. This reminded her of blind dates in college, which she had tried to avoid like the plague. She kept reminding herself that not only was her participation tonight for a great cause, but their boot business would benefit enormously from the publicity. There would be enough women in the audience who had come to see the clothes that she should gain more customers.

Glad she would be in the first half of the

bachelorettes to be auctioned, she left the dressing room to wait with the others. Blinding lights hid most of the audience from view as all the women crowded together in the wings.

Emma Grayson was on stage. Faith's gaze ran over Emma's clinging green dress that fit to perfection. Three men were bidding for a night with Emma, who was a willowy brunette.

When it was her turn, Faith hoped Hank won the bid. Her stockbroker friend wasn't interested in her and it would simply be a pleasant evening. He'd lost four members of his family to cancer and was happy to bid. This was his first choice charity. She studied the audience again, but the lights were too much.

Finally one of the men won the bid for Emma. Andrew LaCrosse, the master of ceremonies, motioned to the winner to come forward and the crowd parted for him as they applauded. A man she'd never met stepped in front of the lights. He climbed the steps to the stage where Andrew met him.

"Our winner, Luke Overland. Luke, this is Emma. Thank you for your bid. Let's hear one more round of applause for Mr. Overland's generous contribution." There was another burst of applause. Luke and Emma waved at the audience and then Andrew directed them off the stage and Faith knew it was her turn.

"Our lovely bachelorette number five, Miss Faith Cabrera," he said.

As the audience applauded while she walked out, Andrew recited her bio. Smiling, she waved at people she could dimly see before turning to Andrew.

"Thank you. I'm happy to be here tonight."

"And tonight you have on a pair of Cabrera boots, made by your family, which has been in the boot business in Texas since 1892. Your belt is also a Cabrera product, as is the leather for your skirt and jacket. Sensational leather and magnificent hand-tooled boots and belt, ladies and gentlemen. We have a great deal to thank you for besides your own participation in this event. A thank-you, ladies and gentlemen, for other pairs of boots and belts donated by Cabrera Custom Leathers for the bachelorettes to wear tonight."

Andrew paused while the audience clapped. When they quieted, he continued, "Let's start the bidding at two thousand dollars. Two thousand dollars, two thousand, what am I bid for Saturday afternoon and evening with Miss Cabrera?"

"Three thousand," called a man and she recognized Hank's voice. Her smile broadened. She was relieved to actually hear him bid. So far the top bid had brought in $8,500, but she didn't care if Hank was the only bidder, because she had done her part for the auction. This would be over in a minute and she would have a pleasant evening tomorrow night with Hank.

"Three thousand, three thousand. Do I hear another bid?"

"Twenty-five thousand," another voice called, causing a loud gasp from the audience. Her smile faltered for a second. Twenty-five thousand! Why on earth would anyone jump over Hank's bid with such an enormous sum? She laughed at the ridiculous bid while the crowd applauded and cheered and Andrew waved his arms in triumph over such a sum for the charity. Then her smile disappeared. It had to be Noah Brand.

"No," she whispered without realizing what she was doing until she heard herself. She wanted to shake her head and refuse, but she couldn't. Her smile faltered again, fading completely this time. An afternoon and evening with Noah Brand. Everything in her cried *no,* but she was locked into this. It had never occurred to her he would bid for her.

She took a deep breath, praying Hank or anyone else might bid. But no one would top a bid of twenty-five thousand. Noah Brand had a purpose; most of the bids were made in fun and by friends or boyfriends. She clenched her fists and smiled faintly.

"I'd say twenty-five thousand has won the lady," Andrew announced. "To do it right, I'll ask. Do I hear another bid? Twenty-five thousand, going...going...gone." He slammed down his gavel as the audience once more applauded.

"Would the gentleman who so generously bid come forward?"

A hush came over the crowd and she knew they were curious to see who had made such an outrageous bid. She wished she could offer more to buy her way out of the evening, but her boot donation had been huge for the company budget and Noah would refuse anyway.

Fury was a flame scorching her insides. She didn't want an evening with him.

And then he emerged from behind the lights and her heart flipped. He took the steps two at a time and crossed the stage to shake Andrew's hand, turning to her to offer his hand, as well. Their gazes locked and her breathing altered and she was again caught and held in his steady stare as his hand closed around hers.

Andrew beamed with joy. "Noah Brand is our generous donor. Thank you both, Faith for participating, and Noah for your gift."

The audience applauded and became a dim noise in her ears as her head spun. "No, no, no," she whispered again under her breath, knowing no one could hear with the thunderous applause.

They turned to leave the stage together. "I am thrilled to win the bid," he said. "However I don't see any smile on your face…"

"You know how I feel about this. You got your wish. The evening will be a business meeting."

"Au contraire," he said smoothly, his gray gaze making other promises. "We'll toss business aside for now. As far as I'm concerned, this can be the last mention of business this weekend." She didn't believe him for a second.

They went backstage to the small desk where a man waited. He held a ledger in his hand.

"Congratulations to both of you," Terry Whipple said. "You've raised an enormous sum tonight," he said to Faith and turned to Noah. "And you, Noah, thank you for your magnanimous contribution for a worthy cause."

"I'm looking forward to getting to know Faith," Noah said smoothly, gazing at her as he replied to Terry. "And I consider this a meaningful cause," he added, and she knew he wasn't referring to medical research at all.

"Good, good." Terry opened the ledger.

Reaching into an inside breast pocket, Noah withdrew a check. He leaned down to fill it in and she studied him while he wrote. His thick black hair had a slight wave. She couldn't see the faintest trace of stubble on his clean-shaven jaw. His nose was straight. His lashes, which were thick, long and curly, gave his eyes an erotic appeal. A constant fluttering sensation when she was near him annoyed her. She wished he would disappear. Instead, she was locked into hours with him. Worse, because of the charity, she would have to cooperate.

"Thank you, Noah," Terry said, smiling broadly, giving Noah a receipt for his taxes. "Thank you again, Faith, for all you did. Now you can spend the rest of this evening getting acquainted. Whatever you want to do—tonight is up to you. It's not part of the auction. But tomorrow at three o'clock, Faith, you need to be available for the afternoon and evening. Most couples tomorrow night will be dining and dancing. That's up to the two of you. Saturday at midnight, Faith, your obligation is finished. Have an incredible time."

"Let's go have a drink and discuss our plans," Noah said, taking her arm.

She knew it would be useless to protest or refuse so she nodded to Terry and went with Noah to the lounge where they sat in a quiet corner booth and she ordered a martini.

"Tomorrow, why don't I pick you up at three? We'll fly to my yacht in the Gulf. We can sail, swim, do whatever we want. Later, we'll have that dinner and dance Terry was talking about."

"In spite of your huge contribution, you have to know that I'm less than thrilled with this prospect."

He smiled with a twinkle in his eyes. "I'll try to win you over tomorrow. Hopefully, you'll have a good time."

The waiter brought their drinks. She sipped the pale liquid.

"So what else is there about you, Faith? Andrew's bio wasn't that much help," Noah said. "Old family, Texas roots. You've been successful in marketing and business and gave that career up when you returned to help your grandfather with the boot business."

She nodded. "Since I lost my parents, my grandfather is my immediate family, so I'm trying to do what my dad did in the business. My late father knew the leather-making part, but he took over the business part long ago."

"I was sorry to hear about your parents' accident—I think we sent a note at the time. You live with your grandfather?" Noah asked and she smiled fondly.

"No. He has a staff who help him. Nice interview technique. I know almost nothing about you, you realize. COO of Brand Enterprises and your family company wants to buy my family's company and we don't intend to sell." She wanted to add *arrogant* and *stubborn* to her list, but she refrained.

He smiled. "Why do I suspect there are some other qualities you'd like to add?"

She could feel her cheeks grow hot at his easy guesswork.

"Ah, your pink cheeks give you away. My only hope is you won't have the same thoughts this time tomorrow."

She sipped the martini, wanting to escape gray eyes that were too intense and a man who was too shrewd. She realized she was up against a formidable foe.

"C'mon, Faith, a penny for your thoughts," he coaxed.

"I'm going to have to do better," she admitted. "You've outfoxed me two times now," she said and the twinkle returned to his eyes.

"I try to get my way."

"You're honest about it. Do you ever not get your way?" she asked, wondering how he saw himself. She suspected he saw himself as invincible.

"Of course I don't always get my way. I didn't when I met you. I wanted you to go to dinner with me Monday night."

"A minor delay. We're out on Saturday night. I'd say you got your way on that one."

"Well, I don't always. But I do more often now than I used to," he added with a smile that was coaxing and she had to smile in return. "Only child—I'd guess you get your way fairly often."

"I might at that," she replied, sipping her martini. "And we're each dead set on getting—"

He placed his finger lightly on her lips. "Shh. Don't say it. We're avoiding business for the weekend, remember?"

Her mouth tingled from his feather touch and she forgot momentarily what she had been about to say. His contact on her lips made her think of a kiss and she looked at his mouth, wondering what it would be like to kiss him. She realized what she was doing and glanced up to meet his mocking gaze. To her annoyance, her cheeks warmed.

"Your pink cheeks give you away again," he said quietly. "And I was wondering the same thing you were. We'll get our answers before the evening is over." He shifted slightly in the chair and his voice became more impersonal, still friendly. "So tell me, what's really important to you in life, Faith? What do you want twelve years from now?"

"Success. Hopefully, I'll still have my grand-father. He's the most important part of my life. Twelve years from now, I hope I have my own family, but if I don't, that's okay, too. So what about you?"

"You can guess what's important to me now. But twelve years from now? Perhaps marrying by then. I hope I've broadened my circle and increased my holdings, become more adept at deals. Simple wants," he said, and she smiled.

"Right. Another billion or so, more posses-sions and your life centered around you."

"Ouch! You've made me sound totally self-absorbed."

"I'm merely repeating what you told me," she said. "At least you're honest about focusing on yourself."

"I just contributed twenty-five thousand to a good cause tonight. That should count for a few brownie points."

"You contributed each dollar to get time with me," she said. "When else have you given that much to a charitable cause?"

"I'm going to have to work hard tomorrow to

change your tainted view of me. Another challenge. You know, about twenty yards from us couples are dancing. Let's have one dance."

Without waiting for an answer, he stood, taking her hand. Amused by his cavalier manner that only reinforced her opinion of him, she went with him. When he drew her lightly into his arms, she kept a discreet distance. Even so, it didn't matter if inches of space were between them. She was in his arms and it was electrifying. Of all men on earth for her to have this volatile reaction to, why did it have to be Noah Brand? He was arrogant, stubborn, strong-willed—impossible. His driving goal was something that would tear up her life and hurt her grandfather. And dancing with him was turning up the heat.

"How did you hear about the auction?" she asked in an effort to distract herself.

"My brother offered his ticket."

"Don't tell me you just happened to take him up on it," she said.

"No. I planned it and I'm glad I did. You smell as good as you look."

"Thank you," she answered. "Flattery rolls off your tongue with ease," she added. He probably poured compliments on any woman he was with.

When he spun her around and dipped, she tightened her hold on him. His smoky eyes held desire. She knew business for him had, momentarily at least, disappeared.

Conversation was slight until they returned to their table. He captivated her with stories about his past until she realized there were few people around them.

She glanced at her watch and looked at him in surprise. "Mercy! It's one in the morning! I need to get home."

"Grandpa isn't waiting. You said you don't live with him and there's no man."

"I got up at three this morning and I got up at three yesterday. I think it's time."

"Three a.m.?" Noah came around to take her arm. "It's past time. Why didn't you tell me?"

"I've been having a good time," she replied with amusement. "Want me to tell you that I was so thoroughly captivated by you that I lost all sense of the hour?"

He grinned. "Maybe that's exactly what I was fishing for."

"All right," she said, looking up at him as they walked through the country club. "I was so beguiled by you tonight that it seems we've been here only minutes," she said. "How's that?"

"How I wish you meant it," he said, holding the door for her as he spoke into his cell phone and then closed it.

She fished out a tag to hand to the valet, but Noah took it from her. "I'll pick you up in the morning and bring you back to get your car. It's late. Let me take you home."

"I think I'll accept that offer," she said, guessing she might have an argument with him otherwise. She should pick her fights, because eventually a big one was coming.

A black limo pulled up and the driver got out to hold the door for them.

Once they were on the road, she smiled at Noah. "Actually, most of the evening, I forgot our differences. You know we're just postponing the inevitable."

He shook his head at her. "Remember, nothing concerning business this weekend. We're just a man and woman getting to know each other."

He hadn't bid twenty-five thousand for her to get a date. She shrugged and watched the houses flicker by outside the window. He was after the boot business and sooner or later he would get to whatever he had in mind concerning it.

She gave him the code for her gated area and they parked in front of her condo.

"How's nine in the morning? You can sleep in and I'll take you to breakfast," Noah said when they stood at her door.

"Nine is fine, but skip breakfast."

"Tonight flew past for me, too," he told her, stepping closer and sliding his arm around her waist. Her heart thudded. Each touch, all his flirting, their dancing, the entire evening had fanned the fire smoldering in her. She wanted his kiss and knew with her whole heart that she shouldn't. He was the enemy. Her anger with him had been temporarily put on hold, and the shadows of the darkened porch kept the real world at bay.

"Faith, maybe the pluses between us outweigh the minuses," he said quietly. He tightened his arm around her waist. She knew she should be refusing him.

Instead, she slid her hands up his arms, holding him lightly, and turned her face up to his. Her lips parted, and then his mouth was on hers and his tongue thrust inside, slowly, causing heat that burst into flames.

Wrapping his arms around her, he leaned over her as she slipped her arms around his neck and returned his kiss. His kiss stormed her senses.

Desire smoldered low inside her. She would regret these moments of forbidden kisses, but she couldn't stop. She wanted him to kiss her all night. Winding her fingers in his hair, she clung to him, moaning softly in pleasure, feeling his erection that indicated he wanted her.

He leaned back against the wall and pulled

her up against him, brushing his hand down her back to her waist. While his other hand wound in her hair, he continued to kiss her.

Her ragged breathing was as loud in her ears as her pounding heart. Even though she knew she had to stop, she couldn't move.

Finally, she pushed lightly against his chest and he paused, raising his head.

His breathing was as erratic as hers and she could feel his heart pounding. While they looked at each other, she knew she'd made an irreversible mistake. She didn't see how she could ever forget his kiss. Or be satisfied with never kissing him again. She should have followed her instincts and avoided his kiss.

"Faith—" He paused and she waited, unable to keep from wanting to hear what he had to say. "I'll see you at nine," he finished and she wondered if that's what he had intended. "It was a great evening."

"Thank you. I think so, too," she said, a tangle of feelings disturbing her. She opened her door and stepped inside, glancing back. "Good night,

Noah." She closed the door and turned off the alarm, peering out to watch Noah leave.

She hugged herself.

Seeing him tomorrow and the evening on his yacht. Her lips tingled from his kisses and she wanted to be in his arms again. She'd had a wonderful evening with a handsome, appealing man—with whom she had merely postponed a showdown. He was irresistible, fascinating, arrogant, impossible and stubborn. As she ran her fingers through her hair, she shook her head.

To her relief, her grandfather had gone fishing with one of his friends and wouldn't be back from the Gulf until Monday. By the time she had to tell him about the auction, which he would ask about, her Saturday with Noah would be over. She was frightened the news of the date would send her grandfather's high blood pressure even higher when she related what had happened.

Why hadn't she seen this coming? She could have gotten a substitute for the auction or just gotten out of it. She truly never thought anyone would make an exorbitant bid to get an evening with her, much less the idea it would be Noah Brand.

Moving automatically, she got ready for bed and lay staring into the darkness, unable to sleep, seeing smoky eyes, remembering his steamy kiss. Fury grew. Sleep wouldn't come. She was hot, disturbed and unable to get Noah out of her thoughts. She wondered how he had fared when he left her. She imagined him gloating over his triumphant evening. She had returned his kiss passionately. It would serve Noah right if he couldn't sleep, either. She had no idea what time she finally fell into a fitful sleep.

Noah's body was on fire with wanting her. She was a sexy, beautiful, passionate woman he wanted to make love to.

He settled against the cushioned seat of the limo. He'd had a far better time with her tonight than he had expected. They would get to business eventually and then it would all be over because only one of them was going to come out of this satisfied. Him.

He looked forward to being with her tomorrow.

To enjoying her before they went back to the problem facing them.

Idly, he wondered whether there was any chance she would skip out on him, but he rejected that. She had to keep her end of the bargain or the auction money would be forfeit. He wanted her in his arms. Tonight she had been responsive beyond his expectations. For once in his life, he was willing to put a business struggle on hold. He was far more interested in Faith as a woman. She was the one he wanted right now.

Sooner or later, he would see to it that she yielded and the Cabreras would sell to him. He couldn't imagine she would be as furious and cold again as she had been when they'd first met.

Tomorrow couldn't come too soon.

Three

Leaving a bedroom strewn with outfits, Faith hurried through her condo when she heard the bell. She picked up her purse, opened the door and drew a deep breath.

"Good morning," Noah said with a smile. Looking relaxed and fit, he stood only feet away. His knit shirt hinted at a sculpted chest while his short sleeves revealed muscled biceps. "You look spectacular," he said, his warm gaze drifting over her bright green linen blouse and khaki-slacks, causing her pulse to jump another notch.

"Thank you," she replied briskly, wishing

she could sound uninterested and cool. "Let me turn on my alarm and I'll be right with you," she said, stepping back to close her door. Swiftly she activated her alarm and then left with him.

As they walked to his car, he took her arm. "Have a good night's sleep?"

"I always do," she said, not about to admit he kept her tossing and turning all night long. "Do you and your brother ever trade places?" she asked in an effort to steer their conversation her way.

"Of course we have. How could kids resist that opportunity?"

"So how do I know I'm really with Noah today and not Jeff?" she asked, knowing full well she was with Noah and not his twin.

"I guarantee, you're with the one and only Noah Brand." He opened the door of his shiny black Jaguar.

His smile was as irresistible as it had been yesterday and she returned it. "So how I can be sure?"

"Want to see my scars?" he asked with amusement.

"No. Forget it."

"We're entirely different. You'll see when you get to know him."

She glanced at Noah. She had no intention of getting to know Jeff Brand or even seeing Noah Brand after this weekend. "I'm surprised your brother doesn't work in the family business."

"Jeff hates the corporate world."

She slid onto the leather seat and waited while he walked around the car and climbed in beside her.

"So you and your brother don't compete."

"I didn't say that. We compete whenever we're thrown into the same activity. That may be one reason he moved on to something else. You don't understand sibling rivalry."

"I'd think with an identical twin, you'd feel as if you're competing with yourself."

"Hardly. I'm not Jeff and he's not me. Don't worry, you're really with who you think you're with."

"I'm not worried. Besides, if your brother's

not with the company, he wouldn't have any reason to be out with me."

Noah gave a brief laugh. "He'd have the best reason of all—we both enjoy beautiful women. Given the chance, he'd go out with you in a flash."

His gray eyes, his infectious smile, his charm—how was she ever going to have the willpower to withstand him? She knew she had to keep focused on his goal of wanting to take her grandfather's livelihood from him.

Noah glanced around, caught her studying him, and one black eyebrow arched. "So what are you thinking?"

The truth was not an option.

"I'm thinking there's no way we can escape the enmity between our families. I don't even know exactly how it all started. I'm not certain if Granddad does."

"The best I can figure was competitive jealousy. My guess is they competed directly in the early days. That's a craft that's been handed down from generation to generation isn't it?"

Half her attention was on his words, half on his gray eyes playing havoc with her heartbeat.

"Yes, it is. I'm thinking how, as far back as I can remember, I haven't heard anything good about the Brands. I'm certain you can say the same about the Cabreras. That feud sits between us like a third person. Our families hate each other."

"That doesn't have to carry over to us. And hate is a strong word. I just want to buy Cabrera."

"I don't think you like us."

"Not so," he said in a voice that sent a wave of warmth in its wake.

"You're not overly fond of Granddad. Don't even bother to deny it."

"The feud can end with us. I promise you, there isn't one cell in my body that has anything except a positive response to you."

She had to smile.

"We have a deal. No business. We ought to expand that to forget the feud, too."

"I'm afraid the family feelings are impossible to overlook. That's bigger than work concerns.

I'll give it a try." She gazed out the window a moment, wondering whether she could even do partially what she said about overlooking the feelings. "You told me you were last on your boat months ago. So what do you do to relax?"

"I work. I spent a couple of weeks in Switzerland last year. I swim and play racquetball. How about you?"

"I spend a lot of time with my family," she replied.

"Sounds as if you're as ready for a day of fun as much as I am. Stop thinking of me as Noah Brand. I'm just a guy today. You'll love it out on the open water and the scenery is great along the shore. We can snorkel."

She laughed. "Fine. Drop your sales pitch."

She had another pang, wishing she had known him under different circumstances. That wasn't the case, and she knew there was no point in longing for something that couldn't be.

He turned into the parking lot of the country club and she directed him to where she had left her car the night before.

After parking, he opened her car door for her. "I'll be by in two hours, and I can't wait," he said, his voice lowering a notch as his gaze focused on her mouth. She remembered his kiss and knew he would kiss her long before evening came.

And worse, she wanted him to. She was torn between wanting to be with him and knowing she shouldn't, and "shouldn't" lost every time.

Ready a few minutes before time for Noah, she called Millie, relating all that had happened. "Did Jeff ask you for a ticket for Noah?"

"Not at all. Jeff took five tickets from me. I didn't know what he did with them. Did you have fun with Noah last night?"

"That's beside the point. Even if he's promised to avoid talking shop, I know he will."

"Forget business and have a blast. You should have a wonderful time."

"Millie, remember what he bid. He was dead earnest about getting this time with me. He has a goal."

"Make him forget it."

"I better go."

"Call me when you get a chance and let me know how it went."

Shaking her head, Faith ended the call. Perhaps the way to do business here was to forget business, as Noah said. Millie's point drove it home further. Promptly on time, Noah rang the door chimes. When she opened the door, her eagerness overcame her reluctance.

"Can I carry something?" he asked.

She had one canvas bag over her shoulder, another on the floor nearby.

He entered, picked up the bag and paused. "Look at that," he said, glancing farther down her entry hall.

She followed his gaze. "My family pictures."

"That's amazing." He strolled toward them. "How many generations back do these go?"

"As far as we have pictures." She pointed to one. "There's my great-great-grandfather standing on a water wagon."

"You are into family," Noah said. "This is a gallery. I can't even tell you my great-great-grandfather's name." Noah moved along to look at more pictures. "Who's this?"

"My granddad when he was nineteen and he boxed."

"I'm impressed. Emilio was a boxer?"

"Briefly, when he was young."

"Here's the Cabrera office years ago," Noah said. "This is interesting."

"It's the same building. Has been since they started," she said, wondering about Noah and his own family. "Family is important to me."

"I guess it is. I don't have any idea if we have old family pictures or not," Noah said. He glanced at her and then looked intently. "Don't look so shocked."

"I just can't imagine. No wonder the old family feud doesn't disturb you. You don't have feelings for generations past."

"Actually, no, I don't. That's history."

"It's your history," she said, seeing a vast difference in their attitudes and beginning to understand why he didn't have such strong feelings toward the Cabreras.

"You just want our business for purely monetary reasons. It's not because of trying to get the best of the family."

"Right." His eyebrows arched. "If you thought I was trying to buy Cabrera out to settle some old battle—no way. You have the finest leathers, boots and saddles. That's what I want and there is nothing in it that has to do with family histories."

She stared at him and shook her head. "I can't understand that. I'm so steeped in family history that it means everything."

"Nope. Just pure business moves me. And ambition," he said, smiling at her and looking again at the pictures. "This is intriguing, I'll admit. I've never even thought about past generations in my family. I don't think Mom and Dad have, either. Which is probably why I don't."

"Well, you've missed something."

"I don't think so," he said. "We'll go, but sometime, I want to come over and have you tell me about each of these pictures."

"I'll do that, Noah. Maybe it'll stir a little interest in your own family. Look, this is a tintype of my great-great-great-grandfather when he landed in New York from Spain. He was seventeen years old and he didn't speak English. He came to Texas when he was twenty-three. I'll tell you about the others later."

"That's a deal," Noah said, shouldering her bag. "Get your alarm." He stepped outside again while he waited. In a minute she joined him.

"We'll be there in no time and you'll be glad we left early. I promise."

"You don't lack confidence, do you?"

He grinned at her as he held open his car door. "You wouldn't want me to be any other way."

She laughed at his ridiculous remark as he closed her door and hurried to climb in on his side, placing her bag in the back.

As they rode, she thought about Millie encouraging her to make him forget business. Could she actually do that? Did she want to? Or would she just entangle herself more with him?

When they were airborne in his private jet, she gazed out the window at Dallas sprawled below. She turned to catch him studying her.

"If you knew us well, now you'd know you're

not with Jeff. He'd be piloting the plane. He loves flying. Probably took up flying to annoy Dad, who worried."

"I take it you get along better with your dad than your brother does."

"Right, but I'd rather not discuss it. My boat is docked at Cozumel. I thought we might have a snack on the plane and then swim before we eat."

Remembering again Millie urging her to have a blast, Faith wondered whether she could forget the generations of family enmity toward the Brands. "You have the day planned down to the last detail, don't you?"

"Loosely," he replied. "You don't look like the 'fly by the seat of your pants' type. Am I right?"

"I suppose, but I suspect your plans and mine for this outing have different outcomes."

"The outcome is a big question mark—that's why we're getting to know each other."

"We're bound to have clashing goals, much akin to the Brand-Cabrera feud," she replied, unable to resist sparring with him.

"I aim to spend this Saturday with a stunning blonde."

"I'm not certain I can get past that you're a Brand. Maybe you can show me another more inviting side."

As something flickered in the depth of his eyes, he inhaled deeply. She knew she was flirting with a handsome Brand, a dangerous path, yet Millie had encouraged a recklessness—or was it Noah who was causing her to flirt?

"This weekend just got better," he said in a husky voice.

"We'll see when it happens, won't we?" she asked in a sultry voice. Maybe she could turn the tables on him, make him forget business and teach him a lesson about mixing business and pleasure. As long as she didn't get herself entangled emotionally.

"My expectations, already high for the weekend, just took a giant leap."

"Your gray eyes give away your expectations."

"And—"

"You'll have to wait and see, Noah. Don't let your hopes run away with you."

"Way too late," he replied, leaning closer to curl a loose lock of her hair around his fingers. "And you've raised them tremendously."

"Noah, you're an impossible flirt."

"I've got the best reason in the world to be."

She smiled at him. "I think at this point we should switch to some harmless topic. What's your favorite pastime that's public?"

He looked amused. "Public—work. If not work, I like racquetball. Now you have to tell me yours."

"Going to the opera, particularly Puccini. Reading. Delving into family history. So what's your favorite food?"

"Steak, definitely, with a bold red wine. Let me guess yours—you look like the baked salmon and a dry white."

"Good guess," she said. "I hope that doesn't mean I'm predictable."

"Absolutely not. Beyond our favorite food, I'm at a loss."

"Impossible," she teased. "Tell me other things you like best."

"What I like—slow, passionate kisses, silky blond hair, big, blue eyes, a soft, curvaceous body pressed—"

"Did I walk into that one!" Holding up her hand, she laughed. "Stop right there. Give me any favorites that do not involve you or me personally. Start with favorite song."

"This isn't half the fun the other was," he replied, still playing with a lock of her hair.

"Fun loses out to caution this time."

"What might make you throw caution to the winds?"

"I think you already have done that, hence my answer would be Noah Brand," she said, knowing she enjoyed flirting with him too much, yet business, for now, had disappeared.

"That's a gratifying answer," he replied.

As they approached Cozumel, the scenery changed with shimmering blue water and tropics below. "This is paradise, Noah!"

"I shouldn't say, 'I told you so,'" he said, and she smiled at him.

"You can say it. You're right." She turned to find him watching her intently again and she forgot about the scenery. Desire was obvious in his gaze, and he had a solemn expression that revved her racing pulse.

"We're going to have a grand time," he said quietly. "As a matter of fact, it's already started. I'll try my best to pleasure you as much as possible this weekend." The double entendre had the effect he intended.

"With that remark, I'd say we need the swim to cool down."

"I don't quite see that happening. Not with you in a swimsuit."

"Just keep your attention on the gorgeous tropical fish," she replied.

She turned to gaze out the window. He placed his hand on hers lightly and she turned to look at him, tingling from his touch. "Stop worrying and having regrets you're with me. It's all right between us so far."

She nodded, knowing even the slightest physical contact stirred desire.

A waiting limo took them to the dock where

they climbed aboard a small boat. In minutes she saw a glistening white yacht ahead.

"There it is," he said.

"That's what you called your boat? It's a magnificent yacht," she said, thinking how casually he accepted the wealth he had been born into.

"It's comfortable. When I'm here, I always think I'll return soon, but then I get busy and forget about it."

"I don't know how you can," she said, realizing she was with a dedicated workaholic. If he jetted off in his plane to relax on his yacht even every few months, it would indicate a man who could leave work behind, but forget about the yacht when he was away from it… No matter what he said, there was only one reason she was here.

When they went aboard, a tall, tanned, dark-eyed man in a crisp uniform met them, and Noah introduced his captain. "Faith, this is Captain Mario Mena."

She shook hands and chatted briefly and met a few of the crew as the yacht got under way.

"Let me show you where your cabin is," Noah

said. "As soon as we change to comfortable boat clothes, I'll give you a tour. In about half an hour we'll arrive at a good place to snorkel. How's that schedule?"

"Fine," she answered and his hand closed lightly on her arm, again heightening her physical response to him. He showed her to a spacious cabin with beige-and-white decor and luxurious furniture.

"This is beautiful, Noah! It's a floating palace," she said. Everywhere they went, all he did, made her wish the circumstances were different and they were simply a man and woman enjoying a weekend and getting to know each other.

He smiled. "Thanks. It's comfortable and I enjoy it when I'm here. Change and I'll be waiting. My cabin is right across the hall," he said, motioning with his hand. He turned and was gone. She crossed her cabin to a balcony that extended over the water. A gentle breeze blew against her, and she inhaled the fresh air and the smell of the sea. Waves washed past below and the cerulean sky held a few puffy white clouds.

Her granddad never took off work, either. She couldn't remember the last vacation he'd gone on, if there'd ever been one. His whole world was his work. In the early days it had probably been to earn a living. Now she knew he enjoyed what he was doing more than he did anything else. She would fight with all her being to prevent anyone from taking that from him.

She returned to her cabin, marveling in the opulence as she hurried to change.

Noah changed quickly to cutoffs, deck shoes and a T-shirt, his thoughts centered on Faith. He had planned this day and evening carefully and if he got what he wanted, she wouldn't return home this night. Never had business been such a pleasure.

She had looked great this morning except the slacks hid those terrific long legs he had seen last night in her short leather skirt. The sparks between them were as intense as ever and he knew she was as aware of them as he was. If he could only keep off business, all would go well. Some women were impressed by his wealth, but he wasn't getting that response from Faith. Something he was unaccustomed to experiencing around any woman who received the wattage of his full attention. Faith was totally focused on protecting that grandfather of hers, and Noah knew he was going to have to conjure up all the charm he could and show her a good time or tonight she would insist on going home.

He was determined to get old man Cabrera's expertise and his boot and saddle business. Brand could market those high-dollar fancy boots far better than they'd ever been marketed before, get higher prices for them and develop the line, as well. Noah's plans danced in his mind.

And if he could seduce Faith in the process— the thought made his heart race. All he had to do was consider the prospect and he was aroused, ready and eager. She was a sensual woman and he'd actually enjoyed being with her enough to want to see her after the dust settled on the business deal.

His father's proposition popped into his head—find a woman he liked to be with and marry and stop waiting for love. That might even be palatable with Faith. He laughed at himself. He wasn't getting tied down in marriage to please his dad or for any amount of money. For once he agreed with Jeff's feelings on a subject.

He left his cabin only to run into Faith as she emerged from hers. His pulse skipped. In cutoffs, a crisp blue blouse tucked into a tiny waistband and deck shoes, she looked wonderful. He couldn't keep from once again glancing at her long, shapely legs. They looked as smooth as silk.

"You look great," he declared truthfully and his voice held a rasp that revealed his response to her as much as his words.

"You do, too," she answered with a smile. "Sorry to keep you waiting, but I wanted my hair in a braid."

"Looks good," he told her, tugging lightly on her braid. "Now for the grand tour," he said.

It was almost an hour later when they finally finished the tour because they had taken their time, stopping to talk and then moving on. "Now you've seen it all. Ready for snorkeling? We can swim in my pool afterward."

"Sure," she said, moving away from him and turning her back to shed her clothes.

Acutely aware of him only yards behind her, she was certain he watched her as she removed her shorts and shirt and folded them. Now she wished she had bought a one-piece suit that had covered as much as possible instead of the blue two-piece cut low on her hips and suddenly far too revealing. Too late now. Then she remembered their flirting on the flight down and she squared her shoulders, took a deep breath and turned, striking a pose.

"I'm ready," she said.

"I think I better hit that cool water," he replied.

She tried and failed to keep her gaze on his. Impossible when his swim trunks revealed a muscled chest, flat stomach, narrow waist and shoulders with bulging biceps.

"I think we both should get in the water now," she said, meeting his hot gaze. He merely nodded and led the way, pausing at the rail. "I had someone take towels and the snorkeling equipment to the beach for us. So first we swim to the beach."

"Let's get you into cool water."

They spent half an hour snorkeling and it was beautiful, but it was impossible to forget the muscled, almost-naked man swimming around her. And she knew he was as aware of her as she was of him. The flames she had experienced all along became more intense. Would the auction that she had expected to be such an advertising boost lead to an emotional upheaval in her life?

Noah swam up and touched her arm. He motioned and they both swam to the surface.

"How about shedding the snorkeling equipment for a while? The water is perfect."

"Sure," she said, thinking it would be good to have a vigorous swim. She returned to the beach with him to drop the snorkeling equipment and then they walked back to swim to deeper waters.

After a time, she stopped, treading water, and Noah bobbed up beside her, shaking water from his face.

"Want to go to the beach?"

"Heavens, yes. I didn't realize we'd come this far out," she said, looking at the dinghy sitting peacefully in shallower water.

"It's easy to do," he said, swimming close and slipping his arm around her waist. Surprised, she glanced up at him.

"Noah," she said, half protest, half invitation.

"This is a memorable place and a memorable moment. Let's make sure it is a special memory," he said and drew her closer against him.

"Noah," she whispered. Her protest was gone the instant she looked into his eyes.

She wanted his kiss, wanted to feel him close against her. Their wet bodies pressed together and her bare leg rubbed his, making her pulse race. He leaned closer, covering her mouth with his.

The instant their lips met, her insides fluttered. She slipped an arm around his waist while she pressed her lips against his.

With a moan, she met his tongue with hers. Her insides clenched and her breath was taken as if by storm winds. His ardent kiss melted her and she held him tightly. Their warm bodies pressed closer, his hard length against her. She could feel his arousal.

The kiss fanned the flames consuming her. She ran her hand over his muscled back, relishing the strength, sliding her hand to his narrow waist. His skin was slippery with water. Each kiss drew her toward seduction. Just as before, there was a dim warning in the back of her mind, but right now, she didn't want to heed it or stop. She wanted Noah as she had never before desired a man.

Shifting slightly, he pushed aside her suit to cup her breast and run his thumb lightly around her nipple.

She yielded to the moment, letting him caress

her, moving her hips slightly against him until she realized how fast enticement grew.

"Noah," she said, wriggling slightly and looking up at him. His smoldering, heavy-lidded gaze made her breath catch. His desire was unmistakable, hot and tempting.

She swam out of his grasp. "We'll go back," she said, turning to swim, all her senses screaming to return to his embrace. Only logic fought and won. She knew she had to put space between them. The past few moments churned with sheerest folly on her part.

Angry with herself for succumbing to his irresistible charm, she swam faster, thrashing through the water and trying to overcome desire that throbbed hotly.

She reached shallow water and stood to wade out, grabbing a towel from the dinghy and spreading it on the sand.

He spread a towel close beside hers and sat, watching her as she sat beside him.

"That kiss shouldn't have happened."

"Nonsense," he replied in a husky voice, running his hand lightly along her shoulder to stir tingles that disturbed her more than ever. "We're a man and woman taking some well-deserved time to relax and escape business. It's the end result of the auction—what did you expect to have happen in that auction? You surely didn't think your friend would be the only bidder?"

"As a matter of fact, I did."

"Look in the mirror," he suggested, smiling at her. "Had I kept quiet, there would have been someone else bidding."

She had to laugh. "Thanks, I guess." She turned to look at the water. "I'll never forget this," she said. "The fish are stunning."

"I was just about to get excited over your remark until you added the part about fish," he said drily, and she smiled again.

"I've only snorkeled once before in my life in a river. It wasn't a good place for exotic fish."

"Ever been in love, Faith?" he asked, returning to something personal.

"Not really. Have you? I think I can guess the answer."

"No, I haven't."

"To me, it sounds as if you don't have time for a serious relationship."

"I can take time for a life. I'm not that much of a workaholic."

"That might be debatable since you can't recall the last time you took a weekend like this," she said. "Do you ever want to get married?"

"Maybe when I'm much, much older," he said, and she smiled. "I'm wrapped up in work and like my freedom," he continued. "I haven't ever come close to being engaged or had a serious relationship. How about you?"

She shook her head. "Not really."

Hoping to cool her desire, she braced her hands behind her, crossed her legs, closed her eyes and leaned back, raising her face to the sun and basking in its warmth.

For a moment she let all thoughts leave her mind and simply enjoyed the sunshine. She opened her eyes to stretch out on her towel and looked over to find him watching her.

"Good heavens, I figured maybe you'd gone to sleep."

"Hardly," he said, his voice a notch deeper.

The moment became tense between them and with an effort, she stood abruptly. "I think we should swim back to the boat."

"Sure," he replied. In minutes they climbed aboard and a member of the crew appeared to take their towels and gear from Noah.

"We can go have lunch now."

"I think I'll shower and change."

She showered, washing off the seawater and drying her hair. After changing to cutoffs and deck shoes again, she went above to meet him.

She had noticed after they left the vicinity of Cozumel, she had seldom seen the crew. All Noah needed was magically done, but whenever he appeared, his crew disappeared. She suspected it was one more stratagem aimed at his ultimate goal of seduction.

After lunch they lounged on deck and then late in the afternoon swam in his pool. To her amazement, he never came on strong again, other than the blatant desire that blazed in his eyes.

As the sun dropped lower in the sky, she'd had

a great time, but there was no Noah Brand in her future and she knew that positively. Tonight when they returned home—and she expected him to try to talk her into staying until tomorrow—she would part with him, and she wasn't going out with him again. Even if she'd had the time of her life with him this weekend, they had no future.

As she mulled it over, she wondered if he would try to pursue seeing her, particularly once he got it through his head that her grandfather was not going to sell under any circumstances.

Going to join him that night, she squared her shoulders and left her cabin, promising herself to remember restraint and try to resist Noah's charisma—he had an ulterior motive.

Four

Noah turned from the rail on the foredeck and came forward to meet her. He took her hands to look at her. "You look stunning tonight."

"Thank you. You clean up pretty well yourself," she said, smiling at him, thinking that was a huge understatement. He looked the wealthy billionaire executive that he was. Being with him all day hadn't diminished the electric current when his smoky eyes focused on her.

"Let's have a drink before dinner. We can watch the sunset," he suggested.

"I'll have a margarita to go with the tropical surroundings."

"We have more reason than that to cele-brate," he said. "Two opposing factions who can become friends."

"Poles apart, yet—" She bit off her words. "Yet here we are together," she finished, wish-ing she could think of some way to change the topic of conversation.

"That isn't what you started to say. Finish what you were about to say."

She felt her cheeks flush as she thought about the volatile chemistry between them. "I did finish it." She looked away from gray eyes that saw too much and wished she had thought before she had spoken.

One corner of his mouth lifted slightly. "Come on," he teased. "You're thinking about the other side of that."

"Don't you even say it," she said more sharply than she intended. "It doesn't matter."

"Ah, I think it matters greatly," he said softly, taking her free hand and rubbing her knuckles lightly with his thumb, causing more electricity to flare. "There's fire between us and you can't understand why. I don't, either, but I know how to enjoy it. And I definitely want to."

Her heart raced with his words and with the movement of his thumb—brushing slowly across her hand with the barest touch, creating the reaction he had just referred to. It was something she didn't care to explore at all.

"No," she whispered, caught and held once again by his compelling gaze.

"Oh, yes. There's way too much sizzle between us to ignore it. This kind of attraction doesn't occur often," he added softly and she couldn't keep from thinking it had never happened before to her.

"You and I are on opposing sides in a corporate struggle—or what's going to be a battle sooner or later. You and I have discussed the enmity between our families that goes back generations. That's a strong reason for us to avoid each other."

"I don't agree. You and I are another generation. There doesn't have to be antagonism and hatred between us. That kind of hatred is taught and it's never directly involved either one of us. I can overlook it easily. That old feud means nothing to me. Now that I've met you, it is even more unimportant. I can promise you, my dad just wants the business for itself. Neither Jeff nor I give the feud a thought. You need to let go. I don't feel animosity toward you, to say the least. Far from it," he added in a husky drawl. "I want you, Faith."

She smiled and shook her head as she withdrew her hand. "The struggle between families isn't going to disappear, Noah, and you can't just ignore it. Whether you like it or not, you and I share that legacy," she said, wishing her answer hadn't come out so breathlessly, giving away that she wasn't nearly as calm as she wanted to be.

"You can't convince me that you really feel that way. I don't and won't ever think that. Watch what happens when we touch," he said, reaching up to caress the nape of her neck.

Drawing a deep breath, she saw his mocking smile while he watched her intently.

"All right, so there's a physical reaction. I still say it's meaningless," she replied.

"It changes whatever is happening between us—I'll spend tonight trying to prove it to you."

"No, don't you try to validate any such thing. I think we'll get on a safer topic," she said, moving a few inches from him and looking around. "You have a band," she said, noticing the men playing drums, a guitar, a bass fiddle and a keyboard.

"A small one, but this way we can dance. They also are part of my crew."

When she stood with him at the rail and watched the sun slipping lower while music played in the background, he turned to her. "I asked what you wanted twelve years from now. What about two years? Same thing you're doing now?"

She shrugged. "Sure. It's interesting. I appreciate working with my grandfather and I hope he's there for a long time to come."

"You don't miss what you did before? It had to have been more interesting."

She shook her head. "No, because I know I'm needed here. I don't think about it. Hopefully,

I have years ahead to do what I want. This is a good experience right now."

"At least you're positive, which makes life better." He gazed beyond her at the band. "Want to dance?"

She went with him to set her drink on a table near his and then they stepped onto the dance floor that they had to themselves. A fast number played and she began to dance, relishing the cool evening breeze that had sprung up.

As soon as the piece ended, he shed his coat and returned to the next fast number. Dancing around with him, she laughed with him when he twirled her, thinking he was incredibly handsome as he stepped with an easy grace to the music. How many times would she regret that he was a Brand, she wondered. Anybody else— but then nobody else would have bid so high for an evening with her. She spun around, trying to work off some of the steam that had been building in her all day while wondering whether he was doing the same.

And then she was again lost in his magnetic gaze, watching him as they danced, feeling the sparks they had argued over and knowing, in some ways, he was right, even though she would never admit it. Desire for him smoldered steadily, changing every word, look, contact. She didn't want it to. She was aware of his body, his sexy moves, his eyes focused on her and holding her mesmerized. Memories of swimming with him, being pressed against his almost naked body, his hot kisses besieged her as she moved around him. An appeal that at any other time or with any other man would have been incredible.

The music stopped and Noah caught her hand, pulling her up against him. She laughed, grasping his arms, feeling the powerful muscles, looking up at him. Her laughter faded, replaced by need as she looked at his mouth and couldn't catch her breath.

Realizing what she was doing, she wriggled free quickly. Then music started for another fast number. As they danced again, that flash of red-hot desire tightened the tension between them, intensifying her awareness of him.

When the small band started a slow number,

Noah pulled her closer into his arms. "I'll tell them to go back to the rock and Latin numbers if you'd prefer."

"Maybe after this dance, but right now it's pleasant to move a little more calmly. I'll catch my breath."

"It's more than pleasant—it's exciting to hold you close," he said, his breath feathery on her temple. "You're light on your feet."

"Nothing like you are," she said, still thinking about him outsmarting her twice.

"Thanks, if you're referring to my dancing, but I have a feeling that's not what's on your mind."

"You're too smart, Noah," she said. He could guess too easily what she was thinking.

He grinned. "Thanks, maybe. It doesn't sound flattering the way you say it. It sounds as if it's a trait you'll hold against me."

"Just annoying to find I can't outsmart you sometimes. And disturbing to realize that you can so easily guess what I'm thinking. You don't even have a sister. You shouldn't be so attuned to women."

"I'm really flattered now. I can't recall ever being told that. Maybe it's my feminine side."

She laughed. "Noah, your feminine side is so buried, I can't imagine it even exists. You're a supremely confident, take-charge male. You're attuned to women because you've spent time with them and are smart enough to pick up on what women like. And I think I'll stop there."

His eyes twinkled while they danced, totally in step as if they had danced together hundreds of times. "And I will leave that comment alone before I hear something I don't want to know, except to say that you, on the other hand, while you may be attuned to males, you're not easily impressed."

She smiled, delighted to hear that he thought she wasn't readily influenced by him.

Later, dark lights switched on, leaving the dance floor only dimly lit by the lights along the rail.

Over a delicious chocolate raspberry cheese-cake, she gazed at Noah. "You talk about college days and younger days, but nothing since. That just adds to my impression that you are totally involved in your work."

As he shook his head, he smiled. "Not necessarily. Just reminiscing, as you have been, too."

"There's no way my life is as wrapped up in work as yours. I'm not as driven."

"You have the wrong impression. This weekend should be some kind of proof that I get out of the office. Ready to dance again?" he asked, and she nodded, welcoming the chance to get up. They had tarried over dinner for a long time.

A faint breeze played across the darkened dance floor, while slow music played. Wishing with all her heart circumstances were different, she walked into his arms as if she belonged there. While Noah had been everything wonderful, there was no way to escape that he was the one man she shouldn't see again. He stood to jeopardize her grandfather's well-being. She couldn't forget the real reason he was with her any more than she could withstand Noah's appeal. Why did it have to be Noah who could make her heart pound and take her breath? He had been right—electricity was the spice of life, transforming their relationship. Right now, she shouldn't be snuggled in his embrace, dancing slowly with him. She shouldn't respond to him, much less find him stimulating, appealing, irresistible.

"See, I told you, the barest contact becomes the most passionate kiss," he said quietly.

She had looked up at him when he first had spoken. Now she couldn't tear her gaze from him, couldn't argue because she was breathless, wanting that passionate kiss.

"All right. No need for discussion. Let's drop it," she said softly, her words sounding more like an invitation than a rebuke.

"Coward," he accused lightly.

"Maybe," she replied with the same amused tone. Trying to end the conversation, she moved closer. His arm tightened around her waist and they danced in silence.

She knew she should say good-night, tell him it was time to start home because their evening together would end at midnight. Instead, she remained silent, wrapped in his arms, postponing the moment they would start home.

Finally, he leaned back. "After this dance, I'll tell the band they can call it a night. I'd like to sit and talk and have a drink. All right?"

Once again, the moment came to tell him to take her home and again, she let it slip past without doing what she should.

Soon they each sat on a chaise longue, listening to waves splash against the yacht while they talked and sipped another margarita.

Finally she stood. "Noah, I really should—"

He came to his feet. "Wait a minute," he said softly, slipping his arm around her waist. "Tonight has been great. We can have more time together tomorrow. Why rush back now?" he asked.

"We're worlds apart on goals. We might as well be facing each other over pistols."

He smiled slightly. "I don't think so. In the overall scheme of things, business differences are nothing. We've already talked about that and you agree more than you are willing to admit." He tightened his arm around her waist. "Faith, I want you here in my arms," he said, and her heart thudded. Her hands went to his waist and her protest died as she looked up and met his heated gaze. Then he looked at her mouth and she couldn't get her breath or reply. Wanting his kiss, she tingled.

"Faith, you have to feel this, too. Have to want what I want," he said softly, drawing her closer.

Stepping into his embrace, she raised her mouth to his as he leaned down for a kiss.

Her heart slammed against her ribs and she knew she was lost.

The time to refuse, to stop him, had already passed. Her insides turned to jelly and she thought her brain already had become mush. All clear thinking had deserted her.

His kiss was forceful, demanding and passionate, dissolving her protests, setting her ablaze. Winding her arms around his neck, she clung to him as her tongue slipped into his mouth. She kissed him with passion, pouring out her desire.

Running her hands over him, she gave vent to her pent-up longing. As she shoved off his coat, he tugged off his tie. Even though she knew she was going down a path she shouldn't, she couldn't stop.

He slipped down the zipper to her dress and it fell around her ankles.

"Noah," she gasped, leaning back slightly. "We're out on the deck."

"We're alone," he said. "No one is on this deck." As he picked her up, he kissed her, silencing any argument or comment and she knew he was carrying her somewhere, but she didn't care where. All she cared about was Noah and his kisses, his hands holding her. She wound her fingers in his thick hair, pouring herself into her kiss, letting go totally.

When he set her on her feet, she realized they were in his cabin. "I didn't know I could want someone this badly," she whispered as she twisted free the buttons on his shirt. His fingers were light, tantalizing, drifting over her, caressing her breasts, traveling down her back and over her bottom. While her bra fell, he stepped back as he shed his shirt. He cupped her breasts in his warm hands and she moaned with pleasure, closing her eyes and holding his arms. She was doing what she wanted. Eagerness to satisfy that ache made her want to remove all barriers.

She unbuckled his belt and unfastened his trousers, letting them fall. Her breath caught at the sight of him.

He was male perfection—flat belly, washboard stomach, lean with muscles. She pushed away his briefs as he kicked off his shoes and shed his socks. His erection was thick, hard and ready.

While he looked at her, he slipped his fingers beneath the elastic of her thong and pushed it off. His gaze feasted on her, roaming slowly over her, a torment as tangible as his fingers touching her.

She knelt, caressing his manhood, taking him in her mouth to kiss and stroke him, hearing his moan until he pulled her up. His eyes blazed with passion and need as he pulled her to him to kiss her hard, possessively.

She returned his kiss with the same fire. She wanted him with her entire being, aching for him inside her, wanting to love him and be loved, give and take from him. This was a night of dreams, beyond reality in the most impossible place and with the one man on earth she should avoid.

"Let go, Faith," he whispered. "Let go and love. Never before—" He stopped and she wondered what he had been about to say.

She knew for her there had never been passion or kisses like his. Her heart pounded and she could barely get her breath. Desire consumed her, causing her to want to prolong the moment in order to take all she could from a once-in-a-lifetime event.

She ran her hands over his naked body, sliding them over his firm bottom, feeling his muscled thighs covered in short, crisp curls. Moving slightly, she ran her hands in the curly mat of black hair on his chest.

"Noah, you take my breath away," she whispered.

"That's my line, love," he answered lightly,

the endearment rolling off his tongue, meaningless and barely noticeable, something she knew
she should disregard. How good it sounded,
though.

He leaned down to take her breast in his mouth,
flicking his tongue over the taut bud while she
clung to him and cried out in pleasure.

He picked her up and placed her on his bed,
coming down to kiss her. His hand drifted along
the inside of her thigh until she opened her legs
for him and he touched her intimately.

He stroked her until she was moving wildly
against him and then he shifted, placing her
legs on his shoulders to give him access to her
while his tongue replaced where his fingers had
been to drive her to new heights.

Need tore at her until she cried out again,
shifting to get her legs under her as she
wrapped her arms around him and kissed him
passionately.

They fell back on the bed and he moved over
her. Suddenly, he paused, breaking off their kiss
as he raised his head. "Are you protected?"

"No," she whispered and he reached out a long arm to the table beside the bed.

"I have a condom," he said, getting one to put it on and she watched, her heart pounding with eagerness. He was virile, sexy. Finally he lowered himself and then entered her.

She gasped with pleasure, closing her eyes as he kissed her and sensations bombarded her.

He filled her slowly, entering and withdrawing, an exquisite torment that heightened her need and pleasure at the same time.

"Noah, I want you!" she cried, pulling at him, running her hands over him, memorizing the shape and texture of him, relishing his smooth, muscled back and firm bottom.

He entered her deeply again, heightening her pleasure. She arched beneath him, crying out for him, wanting more.

"Faith, you're perfect," he whispered, showering kisses on her temple and ear until she turned her head to kiss him.

"Love, I want you," he said, and she dimly heard, not giving heed to his words. Her pulse pounded and she wanted to drive him wild as he was her. She moved beneath him, pleasure building, need overwhelming while she stroked him and clung tightly.

When his control shattered, he thrust quickly. With fury, he pumped and she met him with as much passion. She was damp with perspiration, knowing he was covered in sweat, yet not caring. Her world focused on achieving satisfaction. When ecstasy racked her, she cried out with pleasure. Shaking, while waves of pleasure bombarded her, she held him and felt him shudder.

"Faith, ahh—" She heard his gasp of pleasure as he climaxed and then slowed, his weight sagging slightly.

"Ahh, Faith, darlin', you're amazing. Best, best ever," he whispered.

He gasped for breath just as she did. His hair clung damply to his forehead. She didn't believe any endearments he said in the throes of passion. She was certain he had no idea what he was saying.

Earlier, she had crossed a line and tossed

aside logic and scruples, succumbing to charm and passion. She held him close as he showered light kisses on her temple, ear and mouth and she turned her head to kiss him in return. For now, she wasn't going to think about tomorrow or yesterday, only this moment in Noah's arms, the most exciting man she'd ever known.

His kiss was tender, and for the moment she felt bound to him.

"You're great," he whispered, smiling at her and combing a long lock of her hair behind her ear. Rolling on his side, he held her close, turning to look at her. "This is perfect, and I want to hold you all night. I'm glad you stayed."

"I can't recall giving you much argument on that one," she said in amusement.

"You might not have argued, but you were on the verge of going until we kissed. I'm glad I found you."

She placed her finger on his lips. "Nothing about the outside world tonight. That's my one and only request."

"I'll honor that one. Well, to something more immediate—come with me."

"Why not?" she replied, smiling at him, feeling giddy and bubbly as her hand drifted lightly over his shoulder and back. "You are one good-looking man, Noah."

Grinning, he stood to take her hand. "Thank you, love. And you are breathtaking."

"Such mutual admiration—it's mushy and ridiculous."

"It's delightful," he said, kissing her—a light kiss as he crossed the cabin and led her into the shower.

While warm water sprayed over them, he ran his hands over her. With the first light stroke across her breasts, she inhaled and all the exhaustion and light camaraderie changed. To her surprise, desire was instant and more intense than before.

"Noah," she whispered, running her hands over him as he became aroused and ready.

"I want you, Faith," he said gruffly, pulling her to him, slightly out of the spray of water.

Wrapping his arms around her he drew her closer while he leaned down to kiss her.

Passion ignited, flaring to life as if they'd never made love before. All the urgency returned full force and she wanted Noah with a desperation that shocked her.

She rubbed against his erection, feeling it press her belly and in minutes he picked her up, carrying her to the bedroom where he got a condom.

"Noah, we're dripping wet—"

His kiss stopped her words and she forgot about being wet.

Bracing his feet apart, he picked her up. She wrapped her legs around him, settling on him as they moved together, tension building.

Closing her eyes, she clung to him, lost in passion, moving with him. They loved as wildly as before. She cried out with her climax, feeling him shudder as he reached his. Finally, she let her weight sag against him and he slowly lowered her until her feet were on the floor.

"I'm not certain I can stand," she whispered.

"I'll hold you, always," he said.

"Foolish man," she replied as she turned her face up to kiss him tenderly, still feeling a bond with him that she knew was tenuous and fragile and would too soon be gone.

He picked her up to carry her to bed again.

"Noah, we may be wet."

"I don't think so and I don't care." He stretched out, pulling her close in his embrace and showering light kisses on her temple, lips and shoulder.

"This is great, so great," he whispered. "It's been the perfect day and night—a memory like one of those bright Christmas balls to take out and look at again."

"I'm shocked. The businessman waxing poetic."

"Maybe I have more facets to me than you realize," he said playfully.

"I'm certain I've underestimated you from the first," she said, refusing to think about anything except the present moment.

"Let me see about some of your fascinating facets," she said, teasing him as she ran her hand over his bottom. "Oh, my! This facet is unforgettable."

Chuckling, he nuzzled her neck and she cried out as his stubble on his jaw tickled her. "I'll see what facets of yours I can find and then you'll see what you're doing to me," he said, stroking her bottom lightly, letting his fingers move down between her thighs.

She wriggled and caught his wrist. "Noah, you stop that. You're supposed to be exhausted."

"Surprise!"

She laughed. "You cool it," she said, smiling at him and he smiled in return.

"Ah, Faith, this is good," he said, his amusement vanishing. He leaned forward to kiss her and his tender kiss changed again.

It was dawn before she fell asleep in his arms after a night of loving. Later when Noah's kisses roused her, they made love again.

The next time she stirred, sunshine poured into the cabin and with it came reality.

While Noah slept beside her, her gaze roamed over him. First, memories of the night flooded her. As she stared at him, her problems deluged her, replacing memories.

Looking powerful and strong even in his sleep, he had the sheet pushed low on his hips and one long arm flung across a pillow. Her mouth went dry as she stared at him. Desire stirred, but along with it was anger.

What had she done? What magic spell had he woven last night that she had turned to jelly and tossed aside her resolutions?

Why hadn't she clung to them and gone home? She looked at him again and even though her pulse speeded up, fury burned. How could she have succumbed to him so easily?

Aggravated with herself more than Noah, she slipped out of bed, wanting to avoid waking him, wishing she were back in Texas where she could go home. Furious, she yanked up her clothes. Why had she let him seduce her? Moonlight and margaritas and sheer magic.

In reality, she knew it was more than that. She found Noah spellbinding. There was no way to deny any of his appealing qualities, but they shouldn't have mattered. He was the enemy of her family, her grandfather, their business.

He was sharp, shrewd and determined, and she had known she needed to keep her wits about her all the time with him. Instead, she had spent an intimate night with him.

From the first it had been clear that he intended seduction. When he had walked into the auction, he'd had it mapped out. In spite of her admonitions to herself, her plans and her awareness of what he had been intent on doing, she had fallen into his arms willingly.

As she dressed in green slacks and a green cotton shirt, she wished she could erase last night.

Packing, she struggled to get her emotions under control. She didn't want him to know how upset she was. How he must be gloating over his seduction. He probably hoped she would be putty in his hands this morning, as well as when they returned to Dallas, an advocate for him in dealing with her grandfather.

That wasn't going to happen. Acknowledging mistake after mistake with Noah, she resolved to start using her head.

Finally, packed and ready to return to Texas, she went to look for Noah.

Five

He emerged from the galley. "There you are. Good morning," he said in a warm voice, his gaze appreciative and inviting. "I looked for you."

Trying to ignore the surge in her pulse, she gave him a level look. "Good morning. I'm packed and would like to return to Dallas as soon as possible," she said, the words coming out more sharply than she had intended. It was difficult to act casual and unaffected by all that had occurred between them.

They stood in the narrow passageway, facing each other. One of his dark eyebrows arched and his smile vanished. "Is something wrong this morning?"

"No. I just thought I might get an argument from you. If you're making arrangements to get back—or even better, if we're already headed for Cozumel and your plane, then sorry if I sounded abrupt."

Walking a few inches closer, he studied her intently. "What's wrong, Faith? You don't sound like the same woman I was with last night."

As she banked her anger, her lips firmed. She didn't want to acknowledge the temptation to toss aside her responsibilities and family loyalties. "It's morning. Last night is over and, frankly, even though you're sexy and captivating, Noah, we're still competitors. Let's just forget last night."

"This isn't the reaction I expected." He placed his hand on her shoulder lightly and she frowned.

"Noah, I think enough has been said—"

"Not nearly enough," he stated. "Last night

was a great night and at the time, you seemed happy, too. And satisfied."

Trying to ignore her burning cheeks, she glared at him. "Forget what happened, Noah. Last night is over. We'll go our separate ways. You gained nothing."

"I don't recall being out to 'gain' something. I enjoyed your company, to put it mildly. It was a spectacular afternoon and evening with a beautiful, enticing woman. What occurred seemed natural. It was something you wanted as much as I did."

"I told you that you're a charmer. This is a magical place—I'd had margaritas, my surroundings were a dream. I got carried away."

"I don't recall you having that many margaritas and I know I damn well didn't."

"It doesn't matter now," she said, starting to walk away. He caught her arm and turned her to face him.

"Wait a minute. It *does* matter now. When we return to Dallas, I want to see you again."

"Absolutely not," she snapped, more curtly

again than she had intended. "Noah—we're not going to continue a relationship."

"You can't tell me honestly that you regret last night."

"That is exactly what I'm saying to you," she said, her pulse racing, while a little voice inside nagged that she felt plenty today. "I'm certain you're unaccustomed to hearing that kind of remark, but that's how I—"

He took one step forward, kissed her, ending her conversation. For an instant she resisted, pushed against his chest…

His warm mouth covered hers completely; his tongue played havoc with her desire and intention. Her protests swept away like leaves on a high wind. While his tongue stroked her lips, she opened her mouth to tell him to stop. His tongue thrust deeply as he held her close against his hard length. Her insides warmed. Swiftly, need fanned to hot flames. His hand went to her breast to caress her while he continued to kiss her.

Her thundering pulse was the only sound. Her breathing grew ragged. Some dim protest cried no, but she didn't want him to stop. Wrapping her arms around his neck, she kissed him in return. Her moan was caught in her throat, muffled by his kisses.

Still kissing her, he picked her up to carry her to his cabin, where he set her on her feet.

She wiggled out of his embrace as she gasped for breath. "No! You know you make me want you. There is fire between us. But there is a chasm that's unbridgeable. Don't kiss me again, Noah. Just don't. Take me home. You've won most of the battles between us, but you won't get all you want. I have monumental regrets already. Don't make this worse."

He gazed at her solemnly. "I think you're conjuring up problems that don't exist. You don't dislike me or want me out of your life quite as much as you say, or you would never have reacted the way you did just now. You respond, Faith. If you think I can go back to Dallas and forget this weekend, you're insane. I want you in my arms, in my bed again. We may not understand it, but we sure as hell can enjoy it."

"I'm trying to tell you that we're not going to have a physical relationship. I don't want to pursue this attraction at all," she insisted. "It isn't a friendship."

"Your words and your kisses are sending entirely different messages. I don't believe any of it. You're scared I'm taking your grandfather's company. That has nothing to do with what's between us. I won't pursue buying Cabrera now and I won't talk about it—to you or anyone else with Cabrera, not at all to your grandfather. I'll call off the people at Brand. You and I can pursue our personal relationship without any thought of business. That's a promise."

A thrill rippled in her. She remembered Millie's advice to make him forget business. She had succeeded beyond measure. She didn't think he would keep his promise indefinitely, but he would keep it for a while. The big question now was did she want to pursue a relationship with him, or had this been a weekend fling to make him forget business?

She couldn't see having an affair with a Brand. For now though, she believed what he said. He was still a Brand and that old family feud couldn't be forgotten overnight. Wisdom cautioned her against pursuing a long-term relationship with him. It might be exciting and fun, but her emotional involvement would deepen and the end was inevitable. It could mean heartbreak deluxe.

"I can see why your dad turns the office over to you, Noah. This weekend was a rush to make love. Let's go back to Dallas and slow down."

"I can do that. I don't want to," he said with a smile. "I will if that's what you want."

"It is. This has been a gigantic turnaround in attitudes. You're rushing me and I'm not ready for an involved relationship with a Brand. I'll admit the weekend was special. I can't deny it. Let's have a cooling period with some kind of return to everyday life."

He reached up to caress her nape as his gaze lowered to her mouth. When her heartbeat quickened and her lips parted, she fought her reaction. "Noah," she whispered a protest.

His mocking gray eyes indicated his

confidence and awareness that she wanted his kiss right now. "You can deny all you want, but every inch of you gives away your true feelings. Think about it, Faith. You're taking joy and fun from both of us. Last night was damn special," he said.

She followed his gaze to the bed, remembered too clearly being in his arms, against his naked body. Drawing a deep breath, she tore her gaze away and looked at him again to see an even more satisfied and amused expression on his face.

"Stop fighting what you feel and want," he said softly, running his fingers along her throat. "Your pulse races. You're breathless. Stop fighting it. What we have between us is rare."

"You agreed that for now, we'll cool down."

He removed his hand. "I still want to see you. We'll go home and I'll give you space. This relationship isn't ending. No way can you convince me of that."

"Fine. I'm going above to wait. For now, Noah, the weekend is over," she said, wondering how difficult it would be to stick with her declaration. They both had won what they wanted last night, but what would be the real consequences?

On the upper deck she poured coffee, picked up a faxed newspaper and went to a chaise to sit facing the water. Spreading the paper on her lap, she sipped hot coffee. Shortly, she heard a slight noise and then Noah sat in the chair next to hers.

"Faith, we can at least be civilized to each other," he said quietly. "You couldn't have awakened with bitter feelings this morning. You certainly didn't go to sleep that way."

"Perhaps not as I awoke, but soon I wanted to cool things down between us. There's no use hashing that over because it's done. I upheld my part of the auction."

He studied her a moment and then sat back on the chaise while he drank his hot coffee. She wondered if she had finally gotten through to him about her feelings of caution in pursuing a relationship. Dressed in a tan knit shirt, chinos and deck shoes, he looked like a movie star. How long would it take her to forget him?

Once she was off his yacht and away from him, she suspected it would be infinitely easier.

Even as she made firm resolutions, she had spellbinding memories of the previous night that were still too vivid. Their Saturday together had been a dream come true, but it was one that she couldn't build on or even cherish.

She knew the memories would linger far longer than she wanted, but she could control her actions in the future.

"I'm still a Cabrera and you're still a Brand and I have difficulty getting past that sometimes. That makes me cautious, Noah."

"You know how I feel about all this family history. Drop it, Faith. You did yesterday. Just Noah and Faith. Focus on what's positive and in the present."

"While that's difficult, I'll try. My family is really into the past and family history."

"Have you ever been to Spain and seen where the Cabrera family originated?" he asked.

"No. Traveling there is something I want to do. I wish I could get Granddad to go with me," she said. "A visit to Spain is the one thing I think he might take off work to do. I've considered giving him a trip for a Christmas present," she said.

"What part of Spain is your family from?"

"Southern Spain, along the coast. There are still Cabreras who live there—my grandfather corresponds with them. They still have a leather business, too, although I think it's exclusively horse-based, saddles and harness and that sort of thing. No boots or belts or the articles of clothing we've branched into here."

"Have they ever thought about merging?" he asked and she shook her head.

"They talk about it, but haven't done anything. I think everybody's happy with the status quo. The ambition and drive to grow hasn't grabbed them the way it has the Brands. Granddad is genuinely happy with what he's doing."

"He's a lucky man. Happy with his work, happy with his family. He has you in his life—that should make up a little for the loss of your grandmother."

"I hope I help," she replied. "I know he misses her terribly," she said, unable to imagine that Noah could begin to understand any such relationship. She suspected all his relationships were shallow and short-lived. He would return to Dallas and forget her except for the business aspect.

The rest of the time on his yacht, she stayed in her cabin, knowing she was missing a splendid day, beautiful views and delicious food, but it kept her away from Noah.

Finally he appeared to announce they would dock at Cozumel in minutes.

When she started to leave her cabin, he was waiting and took her things to carry them.

The crew jumped into the docking, and when he reached to take her arm to help her as she stepped off his yacht to the dock, the impersonal contact was as electric as all the others had been.

Soon they were airborne and it was easier to gaze out the window and ignore him.

"We should be flying over some small islands now," he said, moving to a chair near her and close to the window. "I thought about buying one of those islands, but I decided I'd never be there since I'm seldom on my boat."

"Noah, *boat* is a ridiculous word to use when you're referring to a magnificent luxury yacht."

He smiled. "Boat, yacht—it floats and is comfortable."

"You're right about the island, I'm sure," she said, looking below. "You would probably never be there. Besides, an island would be lonely."

"Not with the right company," he said, his voice softening. "I do have a mountain home in Colorado and Jeff has one also. Dad had one, but he sold it a few years ago and neither of us wanted it. My uncle has a cabin still that isn't far from where we are."

"I've met your uncle. Isn't he Shelby Brand?"

"Yes. Don't tell me Uncle Shelby has tried to talk to you and your grandfather."

"Yes, to Granddad, and I was there and met him."

Noah chuckled. "Most of the Brands have

given you or your granddad a sales pitch. Uncle Shelby and Jeff are fairly close."

"I take it that you're not close with your uncle."

"So-so. Jeff's closer. They get along and I get along better with Dad. Jeff thinks Dad favors me and I think Uncle Shelby favors Jeff. Dad and Uncle Shelby have a rivalry that makes anything between me and my brother pale in comparison."

"So your whole family is competitive. My family just has fun."

He laughed and she couldn't keep from smiling, experiencing another pang that Noah was a Brand. If only he had been Noah Smith or Noah Jones or Noah anyone else.

"Noah, you'll have to marry a workaholic like yourself."

"I'm not a marrying man, so that's no worry."

She was drawn into a conversation about his family, learning more about his brother and uncle, seeing rivalry was rampant in his family of males and glad she had no such thing to deal with in her own family.

Again, in spite of her resolutions, Noah entertained her and she forgot she had intended to avoid conversation with him. By the time he drove her back to her condo in the late afternoon, she had warmed sufficiently that Noah was back to flirting with her. The difference now was that he was careful to avoid touching her.

She turned down his dinner invitation and finally stood at her door. "Noah, you know I had a wonderful time."

"I can hear the 'but' in your voice," he said.

"I just want to protect my grandfather and insulate him from being upset. At his age, he doesn't need someone trying to wreck his life."

"Faith, at this moment, I don't give a damn about any of that," Noah said, stepping close to take her into his arms and kiss her hard.

How could he melt her with his kisses? He always did. For only seconds she resisted, but then she wrapped her arms around him, kissing him passionately. Pouring emotion into her kiss, she wished she could demolish him in the manner he did her.

As he leaned into their kiss, his tongue thrust slowly, deep into her mouth, withdrawing just as slowly, stirring a storm of passion and need in her. Resolutions crumbled. Hot, on fire with longing, she held him and kissed him in return. While her heart thudded, she could feel his beating as wildly.

He took her key from her hand and unlocked her door, stepping inside and kicking the door shut as they kissed.

"Alarm?" he asked.

His question finally reached her and she pushed slightly, turning to switch off the alarm. "Noah, just—"

He kissed away whatever she had been about to say. Once again, she clung to him, returning his kiss as he raised her leg up against him to slip his hand along the inside of her thigh. Even though she wore cotton slacks, she burned from his touch and throbbed with desire.

She pushed against his chest and stepped

back, gasping for breath. "No. We're not going back to where we were."

"You want this as much as I do," he whispered, kissing her throat, twisting free buttons on her shirt to push it open. His breath was hot on her nipple through the lace of her bra and she gasped, pleasure streaking in her.

"Noah, stop now," she said. While her words were breathless, weak, he stopped instantly, raising his head to look at her. Desire showed in his stormy gray eyes that had darkened.

"I'll stop, but part of you wants to love just as much as I do. Our loving was awesome, Faith. You know it was. The whole weekend was. I'll never regret it."

"You know I had a wonderful time Saturday," she said stiffly, wishing she could sound more in control of her emotions. She pulled her blouse together and buttoned it.

"Noah, everything went too fast this weekend. I want to step back and take a breather here, at least for a time. Let's take some time and space and see how we feel. Otherwise, we're really rushing into a relationship that could be volatile, given our corporate battle."

"You can't possibly expect me to say goodbye and just walk away now."

"I don't want us to see each other constantly. We're going into a relationship at lightning speed. Slow down."

"I'll slow down," he said, caressing her throat, his gesture mocking his promise. "We won't see each other 'constantly'. I'll opt for often."

She shook her head. "You're impossible," she whispered, looking at his mouth, wishing she sounded emphatic and cold. She knew she didn't and Noah was aware of too much, saw too much, guessed too much.

He turned to get her bags to set them inside. Then he was gone, striding back to the waiting limo.

After closing her door, she sagged against it, exhausted. She ached for Noah's kisses.

"You could lure a bunny to crawl in with a snake, Noah Brand," she said aloud. Annoyance with herself came washing back, pouring over her as if she were buffeted by a tidal wave.

She yanked up her bags and stormed to her bedroom.

Tomorrow she would have to walk into the office, answer questions—especially Angie's—about the weekend and then explain the whole event to her grandfather.

It remained to be seen if she had lost in her battle with Noah. Would he really back off trying to buy out her grandfather? When it came to seduction, Noah had won. She paused in front of her dresser to gaze at herself in the mirror.

"Why were you such a chump? Yesterday and today?" She knew the answer, but she was still angry that she had let sex and magnetism and a hot-looking man overcome her resolutions and logic. When would she learn?

She worked for the next few hours, unpacking, washing, bathing, getting ready for Monday, and then immersing herself in the books from the office until it was two in the morning. Even then, she couldn't sleep and after twenty minutes of restlessness recalling their lovemaking the night before, she returned to her desk for another hour. Next, she switched on an old movie to try to relax and avoid thinking about Noah.

After completing a call Monday morning, Noah found himself staring out the window. He had just told his vice president of marketing that he would handle the Cabrera account from now on himself.

He intended to keep his promise to Faith and forget trying to take over Cabrera. It would be an amazing, lucrative acquisition, but it wasn't as important to him as having Faith in his life. His promise should change her attitude because now they had no issues between them, at least as far as he was concerned. She was far more tied into the old feud than he was. Perhaps that was her grandfather's influence.

The clear, blue summer sky with snowy clouds reminded him of her blue eyes. He wanted her and the weekend had been the best. It was worth losing Cabrera—which they didn't have anyway—to get Faith into his life. She wanted him to slow down his approach and he would back off somewhat, but he wasn't stepping out of her life. Far from it.

His private phone line rang and he answered to hear his brother.

"How'd the weekend go?" Jeff asked. "Was the auction ticket worth the price?"

Noah laughed. "It was a bargain price compared to the weekend I had."

"I'll be damned. You had that good a time with a Cabrera?"

"Indeed, I did. I can trust you not to talk to Dad. I told her I'd back off trying to get her family company while we're seeing each other."

"I think I better sit down. I'm in shock. How will you manage this?"

"You know who's running Brand now."

"I guess you can do what you want," Jeff replied. "Are you really going to do what you promised?"

"Absolutely. It's not that important."

"Man alive. Now I do have to sit down until the shock wears away. I am talking to my brother, right?"

"Don't be a smart-mouth. That's not such a monumental sacrifice because they've always refused us."

"True. You haven't lost anything."

"Not at all."

"And now you've got leverage to get the lady to see you. I never thought I'd see the day you would need an incentive to get a woman to see you."

"I think you're the brother who fits that description."

"So who is moving in with whom?"

"No one at this point. The lady wants a little space."

Jeff laughed. "Wow. Next big shock. But then she's a Cabrera and probably doesn't trust you as much as a mouse would trust a hungry cat."

"I'll do what I say. So how's the ranch?" Noah asked, hoping to change the subject.

"The ranch is doing fine with just the usual petty ranch problems, plus hot weather, and we could use a good rain."

"When will you be in town?"

"I'll let you know. Everything okay with Mom and Dad?"

"Yes, and he's staying away from the office, which is good."

"Surprising, but good to hear. Better go, bro. See you soon."

Noah broke the connection and stared at the phone, thinking about Faith and when he could see her again. He wanted her back in his arms in his bed.

He reached for the phone to call her at work and then withdrew his hand. He'd wait awhile and then call her. She should be back at work by now.

Her busy Monday morning made Angie's questions easy to deal with and there was little time for chitchat regarding her personal life.

Her grandfather hadn't heard about the weekend so far, and she was too busy to bring it up, wondering when he would ask about the results of the auction and how casually she could pass it off.

It wasn't until late Thursday afternoon that

her grandfather stopped in her office to discuss an order for a custom-made saddle and talk got around to her weekend.

"So how did our boots go over at the auction last Saturday?"

She paused in her scribbling of notes about the saddle to look up at him. "I was going to tell you. According to Angie, so far we've received nine orders for boots like the ones that were worn that night. I expect we may have some more orders out of it. We've sold a dozen belts that will be custom-made and two outfits like the one I wore. That doesn't take into consideration the sales we've had of boots and belts through the local department stores and boutiques."

"So it was worthwhile. I hope you had a fun time. So Hank bid for you?"

"That he did. Granddad, he wasn't the top bidder. I should have seen it coming, but Noah Brand won the bid and I was with him Saturday night. He at least agreed we wouldn't discuss business and we didn't."

Her grandfather's dark eyes were always

unreadable. She could rarely guess his thoughts and he was deliberate in thinking things over before he spoke. He sat in silence a moment.

"You had to go out with a Brand," he said, almost as if to himself. She noticed his fists clenched and she worried about his reaction to the news.

"Granddad—"

"It wasn't your fault. Those Brands will do anything to get to us. He won you in the charity auction so you had to go out with him." He shook his head. "They're the lowest."

"Please don't worry. The weekend is over."

He looked up at her. *"So?"*

"So what?" she asked, smiling at him.

"Did you have a fun time? Will you see him again?"

"While I had a pleasant time, I don't know about seeing him again. I've put him off and that may send him packing. I suspect he isn't accustomed to having that happen. I didn't back off completely because he said he's dropping trying to acquire our company."

"Don't believe that one for a second, Faith."

"I know. I'm aware we're still opponents in the business world, so what's the point of seeing each other?"

Her grandfather waggled his head. "Depends, Faith. Do you want to see him again?"

"I can't keep from remembering he's a Brand, so there's no future in seeing him."

"There could be. I could be the one who deals with the Brands on the business side and take it off your shoulders. I don't mind. I've been telling them no all my life. Both Knox and his dad and even that one time, his brother Shelby. I rather liked Shelby more than the others. Not as cavalier and pushy."

She smiled. "No, you don't have to worry about the Brands. Maybe they've finally realized we don't want to sell."

"It's not in them to give up. Has he called you since you returned?"

"No, he hasn't."

"Must not have had such a good time with him, then," he observed. "You said Hank bid, so with two of them, did you raise a lot of money?"

"As a matter of fact, I did. It was a large amount."

Her grandfather chuckled. "Whatever it was, it's way too little for what you're worth, but good for charity all the same. Did he entertain you?"

"Yes, he did," she said, knowing this was the moment to tell him about the yacht, but it was easier to just let it go. "I think I've seen the last of Noah Brand," she said. "At least until he shows up for business reasons."

"Well, if you don't care, then that's fine. I'll get back to what I was doing. How about going to dinner with your old granddad tonight?"

"I'd love to," she said, smiling at him and he smiled in return.

"I'll get you out of here at half past five. My bedtime comes early and you work too late anyway."

She laughed as he left and she returned to the figures in front of her, but all she saw were thickly fringed gray eyes, Noah's infectious smile and his muscled body. She hadn't been able to shake him out of her thoughts. How long would it take?

Six

Noah raked his fingers through his hair, tossed down his pen and turned to stare at the phone. Faith was out there—not that far away. She wanted time and space, which may have been a polite way to get him out of her life. He should be able to forget her and move on, but he couldn't.

How many times a day had he run through his options: He could call her or he could go see her. She had told him she didn't want to see him, but when he had pulled her into his arms and kissed her, she had responded with passion.

"Noah, are you busy?"

He turned to see his uncle standing in the doorway.

"Come in, Uncle Shelby. What are you doing in Dallas?"

"I have to come back occasionally, although London is hard to leave. You haven't been there in a while."

"Too busy here. You know if I go to London, I let you know."

His uncle crossed the office to drape his lanky form in a leather chair. When he stopped to think about it, Noah marveled that his father and Shelby were brothers, because they bore almost no resemblance. Shelby was sandy-haired, blue-eyed, reed-thin, but their personalities set them apart even further with Shelby never taking most things seriously. Noah found Shelby's sarcasm a bit tedious and had always resented slightly Shelby's favoring Jeff, even though they both thought Knox favored Noah. Noah had never known if his dad actually did favor him, or it was simply that Jeff had always stirred up so much trouble that Noah had come out looking like the favored son.

"How'd your Saturday go with the Cabrera granddaughter?"

"Word does get around. My brother, no doubt, told you?"

"The big question is—did you talk her into letting you meet with Grandpa?"

"No, we didn't have a business meeting. We avoided that topic."

"Don't tell your dad. Smart move though, to take it slowly. I guess you and the lady had a good time."

"That we did. Of course, I can only answer for me."

"Well, knowing your father, he'll be hounding you to take her out again to sweet-talk her into selling to us. Heard Jeff offered to go for you," Shelby said, his eyes twinkling.

"Why wouldn't he? She's gorgeous."

Shelby laughed. "You can marry her and get the bonus from your dad."

Noah smiled. "Hardly. How long will you be here?"

"Just came for your dad's birthday party and a few other things. I go back tomorrow."

"You didn't stay at the party long," Noah said, wondering why Shelby really had come.

"I told Knox happy birthday. Well, I better move on now. I know you're busy. Good to see you, Noah. Come to London."

"I will in about two months," he said, remembering the trip was already scheduled.

As soon as Shelby left, Noah went back to thinking about Faith, wondering if he should just call her. When had he last been in knots over a woman? He had to laugh at himself. *Call someone else and forget Faith.* He reached for the phone.

Before he could make a call, his father walked into his office. "Has Shelby been here? He said he was going to your office."

"Yes, sir. Been here and gone now. Just popped in to say hello."

"I wanted to catch him, but I'll give him a call. What did you decide on the Reydon chain? Are you going to let them handle our furniture? What's your recommendation?"

"I've got the figures and the report and if you were pushing for it, I'd say okay, but as it is, I think they're a risk we shouldn't take now. They don't handle top-quality, so why get our brand mixed in with lesser ones? I'm going to say no."

His father nodded. "Good reason. I haven't had a chance to talk to you since the weekend. How'd it go?"

"Actually, we declared a truce and I didn't bring up the offer."

"That's okay if you softened up the woman for later. Are you seeing her?"

"I haven't since last weekend."

"Well, follow up and keep the lines of communication open. She should be putty in your hands before long."

Noah had to smile at such a description ever applying to Faith. "We'll see, Dad. I still have to get the grandfather to listen. He owns the biggest chunk of the company, if not all of it."

"If she listens, he'll listen. Damn stubborn old man." Knox stood. "If Shelby is still hanging around and you see him, tell him to come see me. I'll call his cell."

"Sure, Dad," Noah said, forgetting his father as he left the room. Noah reached for the phone again.

Faith worked late Friday. It was six o'clock that evening by the time she locked the office. She was the last to leave except for the night watchman they'd hired several years earlier after a few undesirable incidents in the old neighborhood.

When she walked outside, Mr. Porter was nowhere in sight. Instead, Noah's car was parked next to hers and he stepped out of it.

"How did you know I work late?"

"Actually, I've been here a while and had to explain myself to your night watchman. I had some work I could do while I waited."

Her heart missed a beat while at the same time, exasperation kindled. "Is this what you call a cooling off?" she asked as he approached her.

He smiled that inviting smile that tempted her

to relax and flirt with him. "You don't look as if you've worked all day and a long day at that. I thought perhaps I could talk you into dinner. You have to eat. I have a place that has food any true Cabrera should like—the best paella this side of the Atlantic."

She had to smile as she shook her head. His engaging grin demolished the protest on the tip of her tongue.

"C'mon. You can fuss after you've tasted the paella," he said, taking her arm and leading her to the passenger side of his black sports car.

"Noah, you are way too sure of yourself. What do you expect to accomplish by doing this?"

"I expect to enjoy dinner with you." He closed her door, cutting off her reply and climbed in his side of the car.

"You're just postponing our inevitable split."

"Why borrow trouble? Worry about a feud when and if one occurs. In the meantime, I wanted to see you and hey! Here we are. Let's enjoy the moment."

She had to laugh again. "You're just impossible.

I'll bet your teachers adored you. You probably had them all charmed even when you were a little kid."

"I did get along with them," he said, making her feel as if her day had just gone from black-and-white to color. "My teachers loved me and I was an adorable student."

"Should I add egotistical to your qualities?"

He grinned and took her hand to kiss her knuckles. "This is much better. I've missed you."

After a swift rush of pleasure she reminded herself to keep up her guard with him. Beneath all the attention and charisma and smiles was a ruthless businessman who had one goal. And it wasn't dinner.

That reminder faded in a whirlwind evening and a delicious dinner. It was almost midnight when they left the restaurant. After getting her car, he followed her home and walked her to her door.

At her door, he held her hand. "I'll come get you in the morning for breakfast."

"Noah, no…it's too much."

"I want you, Faith. In my arms, in my bed again," he whispered.

"That can't happen this soon. I told you, I need time," she said, squeezing his hand and starting to turn away.

He pulled her to him, his mouth covering hers and ending any protest instantly. The moment they kissed, she was on fire. He kissed her passionately, a torrid kiss that racked her with desire.

When he opened her door she didn't know, but they were inside. He tugged away her blouse and reached beneath it to cup her breast and she moaned with pleasure.

"Noah, wait—" She pushed against him and turned off her alarm. Gasping for breath she held out her hand. "No. We're not sleeping together. I can't go through the emotional upheaval of that. Not tonight," she said, barely able to get her breath and wanting to step back into his arms with all her being.

He caressed her throat, letting his hand drift down to her breast. She caught his hand as she shook her head again.

"Ah, Faith. I want you in my arms."

"Goodbye, Noah. Thank you for dinner." Hurting, wanting him with a desperate need, she watched him leave. For a moment she didn't trust herself. Part of her longed to step to the door and call him back and have another night together. The other part knew to let him go.

After she closed the door, she rubbed her forehead, caught in a dilemma.

Noah had promised to back off trying to buy their company to get to go out with her. She felt caught between choices. If she ran him out of her life, the reason for him to stop attempts to buy Cabrera ceased to exist.

On the other hand, if she were to see him while keeping brakes on a relationship, she would give her grandfather a reprieve.

How much was she considering this course for her grandfather and how much for herself? She loved every minute spent with Noah and she might as well face the fact.

She went to her room and was sitting in the dark, gazing out the window, thinking about Noah, when he called. "I thought I'd get a few more minutes with you on the phone before we part for the night," he said.

"Noah, do you realize the time?"

"What difference does it make?" he asked and she could hear the amusement in his voice.

"The difference is that I'll fall asleep in the middle of the day tomorrow."

"Want me to come over and tuck you in?" he asked in a teasing, husky voice.

"Goodbye, Noah," she said.

"Better let me come now. Next week I'll be in Japan and you won't see or hear from me."

"I'll miss you," she said in fun. "I mean goodbye this time," she said and broke the connection.

In minutes she received a text message from him on her cell phone. "Go to bed, Noah," she wrote in return and then climbed into bed.

"I would if you were here," he responded, making her smile and sigh. How easily she could fall in love with him.

The sound of the phone ringing again awoke her. The call was from Millie. She answered, knowing Millie was calling about Noah. She admitted she'd enjoyed the weekend.

"That's great, Faith. I'm relieved. I was afraid the tickets would cause you grief. Are you involved?"

"Somewhat," Faith said reluctantly. "He certainly seems to think so. It wouldn't have been your fault if we'd had a miserable time, anyway. You had no idea the ticket would end up with Noah."

"Maybe, but I would have still been concerned. If you enjoyed Noah, you should stop worrying about business. Besides, your grandfather has held off the Brands before."

"It might interest you to know, I took your advice about making him forget business. As a result, he says he is backing off the buyout."

"Awesome," Millie replied.

"I'm not rushing into a relationship, but right now, Noah is in my life."

"Even more awesome. Now I can stop feeling guilty about that ticket."

"You definitely can," Faith remarked drily. "How are things going with you?"

She listened and chatted, relieved that they didn't return to talk about Noah and shortly she said she had to go.

"Relax and enjoy Noah. Half the single women in town would trade places with you in a flash if they had the chance."

Faith smiled as she said goodbye, thinking about Noah and their time together earlier.

By the seventh of April, she had been feeling sick every morning and then fine the rest of the day. She had started to worry because she had missed her period.

Friday, nauseated once again, she studied the calendar. Noah had used protection, but that wasn't absolute. Worried, yet feeling ridiculous, she left work to get a pregnancy test kit and returned home to use it. While she waited, worry was impossible to avoid. She couldn't bear to consider the future yet. Not until the results were in.

Stunned, she stared at the results. A baby! She was pregnant with Noah's baby. Her plans for her future went up in smoke. She was going to have a baby. A Brand baby. Her head swam and she stared into space unable to move or think for a few moments while her initial shock diminished.

Fury came first, followed by a chilling fear that Noah would somehow use the baby to exert control over the company.

If they married, it would be impossible to keep him from gaining control of part of the family business at some point in time.

Under no circumstances could she marry Noah. Her grandfather would never accept him. She knew how deeply ingrained her grandfather's hatred of the Brands was.

The two families might as well have been feudal all these years. How would she break this news to her grandfather?

He hadn't taken it well when she'd had to tell him that Noah Brand had outbid everyone for her at the auction. If Noah winning her in a charity auction for one evening out with him had made Granddad angry, this news would be catastrophic.

She knew she could only blame herself. She

had been the careless one, the one who had succumbed to Noah's charm, the one who had been seduced.

For the rest of her life she would have Noah's child and her family's lives would be tied to Noah and the Brands. The unthinkable had occurred.

She put her head in her hands and cried, giving vent to her frustration and shock. Finally, she decided tears would not offer one shred of a solution. She washed her face and called for an appointment with her doctor, who worked her in that afternoon.

The visit brought official word that she was pregnant.

She had always wanted to have a family, but this wasn't what she'd had in mind. She also had a vision of what marriage should be—the kind of relationship her parents and grandparents had had—one with trust, respect, love and companionship. Friends and lovers.

She and Noah had been lovers briefly, friends, not at all. When you got right down to it, she barely knew him. She had never met his father or brother, never seen Noah's home. Nor did she want to. Noah was such a totally take-charge man that she wanted to have some things set in place before she informed him that he was a father.

And what a hold Noah could gain over the company if she married him.

Cold with worry, she had to chart a course of action to deal with Noah.

She rubbed her temple. What a muddle she had gotten herself into. Would her grandfather love her baby? Since it was a Brand, she couldn't answer her own question.

She would have to tell people closest to her—Angie, who worked with her daily. It wouldn't be long before some of the more observant around her would guess.

The following Thursday, Faith chose a moment when she was alone in her office with Angie. "Close the door. I need to talk to you about something."

"I wondered when you would," Angie said, closing the door and returning to sit across from her.

Surprised, Faith studied her receptionist. "You've guessed."

"Yes. One of my younger sisters lived at home when her first two babies were born."

"I'm amazed, Angie. I was slow to catch on. I've been around my aunts, but I guess I paid little attention to what they went through."

"You have morning sickness. Otherwise, are you all right, Faith?"

"Physically, yes. I'm still in shock. This pregnancy wasn't in my plans. I have to tell Granddad. You're the first. I have a feeling you're going to be the easiest."

"Your grandfather is levelheaded. I've never seen him lose it. Anything I can do, just let me know."

"The father doesn't know and I don't want him to know yet. He'll try to take over."

"So it is Noah Brand. Wow. I figured it had to be. I haven't seen Hank around for a long time. But you guys were always just friends, no?"

"Yes, I don't want to tell Noah this early."

"Just remember, you have friends, your grandfather and all your other relatives. You won't be alone in this."

"I know I won't," Faith replied. "This just isn't what I'd planned. I think I'll go home early today. I'll tell Granddad that I'm going home and then I'm leaving."

"Sure. I'll cover here and I can send your calls to your cell phone if it's something important."

"Thanks, again, Angie."

"Any time you want to talk, I'm here," she said and they smiled at each other.

Faith glanced at her watch and saw it was almost four.

She called Noah to tell him something had come up in case he planned to drive by.

When she replaced the phone onto the receiver, she intended to make some plans quickly. Noah was present too much to put off seeing her for long.

The day had taken a toll on her and she felt she needed some solitude to think about her future.

In warm April sunshine she drove away from

the office. She had made plans to eat dinner to-morrow night with her grandfather. Afterward, she would break the news to him. She prayed to discover a Brand great-grandbaby wouldn't be too great a blow.

After dinner Friday as she sat in her grand-father's comfortable family room, she looked at the surroundings that had been her first memories as a child. There were pictures of her at different ages still on the bookshelves, dog-eared books that she had delighted in as a child, even a few that her grandmother had read to her often. She had loved to stay in this house and she still was comfortable here, thinking of it as home as much as the house where she grew up.

Several times now sadness had enveloped her because her parents would never know their grandchild. She felt her father would have been able to accept a Brand baby better than her grandfather, who grew up with some of the actual battles between the two families. Her mother would have loved a grandchild.

Her grandfather would be a whole different matter.

He had on his slippers and sweater and was pushed back in his recliner with a hot toddy in his hand. He smiled at her and she crossed the room to pull a chair near him.

"I have some news for you," she said, taking his hand.

"I hope it's good news. It must be," he said, his dark eyes focused on her. "You don't look down in the dumps."

"It's something unexpected and it's taken me a few days to get accustomed to the idea. Before I told you, I wanted to think things through. I hope you don't get angry."

"Angry at you? Of course, not. Look, sweetie, if they want you to come back to your old job, we can manage," he said and she smiled at him, patting his hand as she shook her head.

"No, Granddad. They haven't called me to come back and even if they did, I'm happy here."

"Well, now I am curious. I'll stop guessing and let you tell me."

"Maybe you better take another little sip of your drink."

He smiled at her. "That bad, huh?"

"You're going to become a great-grandfather," she said, holding her breath and waiting to see what his reaction would be.

"I may need a sip of my drink," he said, frowning and gazing at her with a thoughtful expression. "Are wedding bells ringing anytime soon?"

She shook her head. "No. This baby was a surprise. But I figure that with you here, I'll get along."

"Well, I'll be damned," he said. Setting his drink on the table near his chair, he pulled her to him to hug her. "Of course I'm here. Great-grandfather!" He released her and looked at her intently. "How do you feel?"

"I'm having a little morning sickness and the doctor said that should pass. Otherwise, I'm fine. I was surprised because this was unexpected, but I'm beginning to adjust to the idea. As I said, I have you here and I think I'll be all right."

"You can move in with me if you want," he said.

She smiled and hugged him again. "Thank you. I'll keep that offer in mind, but I don't think you'll want a baby crying all hours of the night."

"You think I haven't heard one before? Besides, now I can take off my hearing aids and let you deal with your little one. You move here if you want, even if it's just a couple of months."

"Thank you," she said, scooting back on her chair. "I love you and I knew you'd be—I guess *supportive* is the right word."

"Why won't there be wedding bells? Does the father know?"

"I haven't told him. I wanted to tell you first. This may be more difficult for you."

He stared at her. "Dammit, it's Noah Brand, isn't it?"

She closed her eyes and nodded, opening them again. "You guessed."

"I think that's the only man you've been out with recently. Dammit. You didn't even know

Noah Brand before the auction. You've just handed him our business on a silver platter," he snapped and struck the arm of his chair.

Her stomach knotted because she had upset him badly. He never used harsh words with her.

"I won't, Granddad."

"He can damn well marry you and give this baby his name."

"I don't want to marry him. Our families have never gotten along. You don't like any of the Brands and vice versa."

Her grandfather stood and moved to the mantel, glaring fiercely into space while he took another long drink. "I don't like it, but I think you should marry, Faith. This is his responsibility, too. Marriage would give your baby his father's name and guarantee support."

"I'll give the idea consideration," she said, hoping that would satisfy her grandfather.

"I want to talk to him. Since your dad's gone, this is my place."

"No, no," she said, rubbing her brow and feeling her stomach churn at the new request. "You insisting Noah marry me isn't what I want. Please, no. Just leave Noah to me, Granddad," she said, wishing he hadn't known who was the father.

"Faith, he's going to marry you."

"Granddad," she persisted, growing more concerned by the minute. "Please, times have changed. Women have babies and don't get married—"

"Not in my family," he snapped.

"Just wait. Give me time to deal with Noah. We have nine months—almost a year, so I don't want to rush into anything. Please, please, for my sake, promise me you'll wait and let me deal with him. I'm begging you on this."

He studied her, set his drink on the mantel and walked over to place his hands on her shoulders. "Stop worrying. The last thing I want to do is upset you. I'll wait a short while, I promise, but he better stay out of my sight."

"Don't do anything rash. I don't want Noah to propose to please you. There's no love between us. It was a romantic weekend, but we're not in love. I want love in a marriage."

"Look here, Faith. I may be old-fashioned, but our family has values and this baby's father should recognize and support his child."

"Just give me time with Noah. This is not what I wanted to happen."

"I'll give you a little while."

"Thank you." She was relieved for any delay. Now there were two men in her life she had to deal with.

"Stop looking worried. I love you and want what's best for you," he said.

"Thank you. I need your love, not more problems."

He nodded with a somber expression and she guessed she had only a short reprieve. She prayed she could keep the two men apart.

It was already past the hour her grandfather usually went to bed. She moved away.

"I'll tell your grandma tonight when I pray. Those aunts of yours all love babies. So do their kids, so you won't be alone. You take good care of yourself."

"I'm fine. I'm going home. It's late and I do get

tired more easily now. I know you're probably tired, too."

He walked to the door with her and kissed her on the cheek, giving her another hug. He stood in the doorway until she was in her car and she watched him close the door. She prayed he would keep his word and not talk to Noah anytime soon.

Her grandfather's initial reaction had revealed his deepest feelings. Telling her she had given their business to Noah would stay in her memory a long time. That was her own big fear. Now Noah had a tie to the Cabrera business that gave him power. He had leverage through this baby to make her cooperate.

She would have to deal, too, with her grandfather's old-fashioned values.

She couldn't imagine her grandfather trying to force Noah into marriage. She remembered Noah saying he wasn't a marrying man. She shuddered at the thought, determined to avoid that as much as any proposal from Noah. She would decide when and where and how she would break the news to him. If she could have a month before she told him, she should be able to make decisions about her future.

She no longer had the option to get Noah out of her life, so she was going to have to deal with him on some level. It was a change in her views of him, but one that had to happen. The idea made her insides fluttery. She didn't want marriage without love, yet her future was different now. She had to think of their baby. *Their* baby. Would she ever grow accustomed to the situation?

She had to tell Noah soon. The thought made her palms grow damp. She was excited by Noah, attracted to him, yet at the same time, her life had always revolved around her family and their history. Everywhere she turned were objects that held sentimental value for her and the rest of her family. Her condo held them. Her office did. Her grandfather's home and her parents' home. All her aunts and cousins. From the old buildings that were the original office to the latest pictures of her grandfather, she was tied into her family heritage, which included generations with hatred of Brands.

During the weekend with Noah, she had tossed all that aside for one magical night. Could she get beyond family history on a permanent basis? Could she accept Noah as if his last name wasn't Brand? She had to try.

If Noah was eager to marry, it would be with an ulterior motive. A way to get the business. And she really had given it to him eagerly. That was the one thing that she had to protect in some manner because it was her Granddad's livelihood and love.

When she left the office after work Monday evening, Noah was waiting. With a prickly awareness of her condition, she drew a deep breath.

"I've missed you," he said, walking up to kiss her. She had mixed feelings about him. Now they were stronger and more divisive. She returned his kiss briefly.

"There might be better places than here. Mr. Porter is around here somewhere, patrolling the premises and if he isn't, we could get mugged out here."

"If that's the case, you shouldn't be leaving

here alone. I'm surprised your grandfather hasn't fussed about that."

"Why do you think we have Mr. Porter? Besides, he thinks I leave by half past five."

"Well, I don't think you should be leaving so late. Where is this Mr. Porter you're always talking about? I rarely see him."

"He's here," she replied. Noah held the passenger door open in his sports car. She jiggled her keys at him.

"I think I'll take my car. I have a busy morning tomorrow."

"Don't be ridiculous. I can get you to work on time," he said, smiling and taking her arm. "C'mon."

"Noah, you don't understand the word *no*."

"Sure I do. I just don't like it," he said. His fingers were light on her arm, moving her toward his car, and she climbed inside.

She watched him walk around the car. In his charcoal suit, he was handsome and commanding. Out of the clothes, he was breathtakingly sexy. The perfect male in some ways, but his loyalties would forever divide them. Yet for the father of her baby, she couldn't have a better candidate. Noah was smart, good-looking, fit, charming, successful, driven—many good things.

He sat beside her, turned the key and glanced at her, his gaze intent and unnerving.

Uneasy, she tilted her head. "What? Why are we just sitting here?"

"You're studying me as if I'm a bug beneath a microscope. I think I'm the one who should be saying 'what'."

She placed her hand on his knee to distract him. "Don't be ridiculous. Would you like to get takeout to go to my condo? We'd have a private evening."

"That sounds like the best idea I've heard all day. How about a rib dinner? I know the number of a place that has great barbecue."

"Fine."

As usual, his gray eyes were unfathomable. She could no more guess what was going through Noah's mind than she had ever been able to guess her grandfather's thoughts.

When she moved her hand away, Noah took it

and placed it back on his knee. "That's better," he said.

"I just wanted your attention," she said, starting to pull away again, but he enclosed her hand with his. She could feel the warmth of his leg through the thin wool of his trousers. "Noah, put your hands on the wheel. You're driving."

"We're at a red light. At green, I'll be the model driver," he teased, caressing her thigh and making her want him more by the second.

"We have a green, so stop teasing me."

"Ahh, so you notice. We could do something about your torment. It can't be half as great as mine."

He moved his hands to the wheel.

"Tonight, I'll give you the grand tour and some family history. Want to hear about the Cabreras?"

"Can't wait. Particularly one Cabrera."

Her attention was only half on their lighthearted conversation. She enjoyed Noah. Again she realized how easy it would be to accept him if she could get past her history. Noah had never done anything to her family, nor had his dad.

Even so, it was difficult to drop dislike that had been instilled from her first memories.

When they finished eating, Noah helped her clean. He had shed his coat and tie and unfastened the top buttons of his shirt. He flirted and teased and she responded, knowing the fires between them were building, yet letting go some of her reluctance to respond to him.

"Come learn some Cabrera history and broaden your horizons, Noah," she said, taking his hand. His fingers laced through hers and he pulled her close against him when they stopped in the front hall.

"I'll skip explaining all the baby pictures and just tell you about ones that I think might interest you. Here's my great-grandfather working in the shop and my grandfather standing watching when he was a little boy." She pointed to a picture, glancing at Noah as he studied it.

"That's a great picture to have," Noah said, sounding genuinely interested. "I don't know if we even have any old pictures. My mom is into shopping and travel and Dad was never into stuff like this."

"Here's another one you might find interesting."

"Cool," Noah said, moving on to a picture of her grandfather.

"Granddad is showing off the first pair of boots he made all by himself. He still has them—he can't wear them any longer and they're pretty worn, but he still loves them."

"Don't blame him. He looks like he's fourteen years old."

"No, he was sixteen," she said, aware of being pressed against Noah's side. He had released her hand and draped his arm across her shoulders. "See why I'm so steeped in family history? Holidays, Granddad's house or wherever we congregate is filled with family, every relative we can round up."

Noah turned to look at her as she talked. His gray eyes were an invitation, his mouth too tempting. While she wanted to explain herself to him, part of her was remembering his fiery kisses.

"I don't think you have anything like that in

your family. No history, no contemplating the past, no strong feelings about the feud."

"That's right. I'm beginning to see where you're coming from about the old family quarrel, but you need to take a long look beyond all that. I still say it's history. You can put it behind you."

"I'm trying to, Noah," she answered, meaning what she said. "I know I have to."

"Faith, I've missed you like hell," he said, drawing her closer to kiss her.

Desire replaced all else as she wrapped her arms around his neck and kissed him in return. He was the father of the baby she already carried. She needed to accept him into her life and see where it led. He had vowed to back off business. Now she would see if he meant it and would keep his promise.

If he hadn't said a word to her about missing her, his kiss would have conveyed the message. She felt wanted with an intensity that surprised her. Noah groaned, running his hand lightly over her, caressing her back and nape, sliding his hand over her bottom while he held her tightly with his other arm.

He raked his fingers in her hair, spilling pins, letting locks tumble over his hand while he showered kisses on her throat and ear and then returned to her mouth.

She pressed against his hard length, relishing being in his arms, feeling it had been an eternity since that weekend they'd spent together.

The urgency she felt also shocked her. Was part of it the realization that she was going to have to let go of the past? She ran her hands through his thick hair, relishing touching him, kissing him, wanting all of him. She stepped away to unfasten his buttons and run her hand over his chest, caressing him as they kissed.

She didn't notice his fingers at her buttons until her blouse fell away, followed by her skirt dropping around her ankles. She longed to touch, kiss and explore. She wanted to make up for the nights alone when she had dreamed of him.

"That is what's real, darlin'," he whispered. "Not all that past between our families."

Her entire being was focused on loving Noah. While the problems temporarily fell away, desire burned with golden flames.

He picked her up. "Where's your bedroom?" he asked. She motioned before he kissed her again and she closed her eyes. As she wrapped her arm around his neck, she forgot what he'd asked. She wanted to kiss him for the rest of the night.

When he stood her on her feet, he continued to kiss her. His hands played over her, caressing her, touching her intimately, heightening desire.

Her dreams were coming true this night. She had longed for him, struggled to get him out of her thoughts. Now she could love him and eagerness made her hands shake. As she showered kisses on him, he grasped her shoulders. She heard him inhale deeply and then he pulled her to her feet to kiss her passionately.

He leaned down to kiss each breast while his hand slipped between her thighs to caress her.

"Noah, I want you," she said, tugging at his shoulders.

"You can't know how much I want you," he whispered, making her heartbeat skip. He leaned away to look at her slowly, his gaze almost as tangible as his touch. "You're beautiful, darlin'." He picked her up to place her on the bed, then turned to get protection. She didn't stop him. Not yet. He didn't know it wasn't necessary and this wasn't the moment.

She opened herself eagerly for him, wanting him. They moved together with the tension building between them.

He maintained control, loving her and heightening her pleasure until she spilled over a brink to reach her climax. As he pumped faster, he shuddered with his release.

"Faith, ahh, darlin', this is the way it should be," he whispered.

She felt as if she were falling back into reality from rapture. His weight lowered slightly and she held him close, shutting her mind to problems. This intimate moment wasn't the time to reveal the baby to him. She wanted the closeness, the harmony they were finding right now. They might need it later.

"This is better," he whispered, kissing her ear and throat, rolling over and taking her with him so he could face her. He brushed her hair away from her face. "I've missed you more than you can imagine."

While she ran her hand over his chest, she tangled her fingers in his chest hair. His chest was rock hard, muscular. "You have to work out sometime, Noah, to have all these muscles. You're in the office long hours. When do you work out?"

"Early usually. I get up, spend about an hour," he answered between light kisses on her temple and ear and throat. "Faith, this is special. I've dreamed of this. I want you with me. Stop holding me at arm's length."

"I will," she answered, wondering about their future while she wasn't ready to deal with it yet.

"Excellent," he said in a husky voice, as he combed her hair away from her face with his fingers. "If I can back off trying to buy your business, you can ease away from clinging to the past," he said.

"I'm trying, Noah. That isn't something you can switch off the way you would a light."

"I understand," he replied while still showering kisses on her.

She shifted to hold his jaw with one hand. "Noah, remember this night. Everything is harmonious between us. It's fine right now."

"And it'll stay that way if we both want it."

"We'll see what tomorrow brings."

"You in my arms I hope," he said, pulling her close to hug her, and then he shifted to kiss her lightly on the mouth.

They loved through the night and Noah felt as if he were in paradise. He wanted her in his life more and this night just reinforced his feelings for her. If he could just get her to relinquish the generations of bitterness over the feud, they could have a relationship. He thought of her long entry hall that was lined with family pictures. She did cling to the past and to family. He cared for his parents and his twin, but he hadn't even known one set of grandparents—only one grandfather whom he found to be rather stern.

His views of the past were fuzzy and un-important. Tonight she'd been able to let go, so perhaps that was a good sign of things to come.

He pulled her closer against him, relishing her soft curves that set him ablaze so easily. He wanted her more than ever now. There had to be some way to get her to overlook the past and stop worrying about his motives toward their family business. Maybe tonight was an indication she was letting go and beginning to trust him.

No one could bypass him to go after buying Cabrera, and he intended to honor his promise to her as long as they were having an affair. He thought about her family pictures and how deeply she was into family. This was a woman who would never take an affair lightly and he did not want a serious commitment. He wasn't into marriage and he had always planned to marry after he was into his forties—years from now. That might be a drawback with her. If so, he knew it was a big one.

Noah shifted to his side, holding her close as he kissed her lightly and caressed her, waking her to love again.

In the early light of dawn, Faith snuggled close against Noah. "You've never even had a full tour of my condo, much less looked at all the things I intended to show you from other generations of my family."

"We'll save it all for another time," he said, kissing her temple lightly. "I'll meet you after work tonight. It's your turn to see my place. Come home with me after work."

"Fine. I'd like that," she answered, knowing she should see where he lived. She was going to try to let him into her life, which he seemed to want to do. She didn't know him well enough to guess what kind of reaction he would have when he learned he would become a father. The need to tell him nagged at her more strongly.

"In the meantime, we need to get up, Noah."

"I'll tell you what's up," he teased and rolled on top of her to kiss her.

She told him goodbye after seven, watching him drive away before she closed the door. She had let him back in her life and there were hours when she forgot he was a Brand. She didn't know where they were going with their affair and couldn't guess how he would react when he learned the truth. Yet she felt she might be moving in the right direction to try to lose some of her distrust of his family. All her animosity vanished completely when she was with Noah. Yet it wasn't going to change her grandfather's feelings. That was another hurdle. Before too much longer, she had to tell Noah about the baby. Noah was amazingly perceptive.

Seven

"Good evening, Mr. Porter," Noah said, stepping out of his car and dropping his keys in a navy suit pocket. "I'm glad to see you on duty. I worry about Miss Cabrera working at night."

"I'm always here and should I get sick, I have a substitute," he said, flashing a badge to open the locked back door for Noah.

"Thanks." Noah walked down the hall toward her office. "Faith," he called.

She thrust her head out of her office and stepped into the hall. "How did you—" She stopped. "Mr. Porter let you in, didn't he?"

"Don't tell him not to," Noah said, amused

that she sounded annoyed. If she weren't so responsive to him, he would have given up long ago, but there was the other side of their relationship that indicated she wanted to be with him as much as he wanted to be with her. Last night she had been warm, friendly and passionate. Now she seemed to be back to her prickly self.

"You're early, Noah," she said. "I need to close up." She hurried into her office and he followed, looking around and stepping to the saddle.

"What's this?"

"My great-great-grandfather's saddle that he made and used. I told you we are really into family and the past, which you aren't. You aren't into marriage. You're not into long-term relationships, you've said so yourself."

"Stop quoting things I've said. There's always a first time. Let's explore what we have," he said, walking up to her and placing his hands on her shoulders. To his satisfaction, as he caressed her throat, he could feel her racing pulse.

"This is what keeps me coming back even when you tell me we have no future together.

Your pulse is racing and you're breathless. I can see desire in your eyes—the same that I feel. We have fire and passion between us. Stop fighting me," he urged.

"Oh, Noah," she said in exasperation, but then she looked at his mouth and her lips parted. He leaned forward to kiss her, pulling her close, pressing her soft curves against him while his heart pounded. He wanted to take her right here in this office.

He kissed her, sending the temperature soaring. Her lips were soft, inviting. She was all softness and curves and silky skin, sweet-smelling, seductive. He was aroused, aching for her, wanting to be rid of the clothes between them.

"Noah," she said, pushing against him. His pulse pounded, making her voice dim. He raised his head, framing her face, not trusting his voice. Her eyes had darkened with passion and her mouth was red from his kisses. He wanted to bury himself in her softness, to caress and kiss her. He inhaled deeply, trying to get himself under control.

"If you're ready, we'll go to my house," he said in a husky voice. "Where's your purse?" he asked, kissing her ear and stroking her back while he held her lightly.

She turned away, walking around her desk to turn off her computer. Trying to cool down and get his mind off sex with her, he glanced around. Looking at her office, he moved restlessly. On the edge of her desk was a book and he stepped closer to look at a smiling baby's picture. She grabbed the book and dropped it into a drawer.

Her cheeks were flushed and her eyes bright. "What was that?" he asked, wondering why she had put it away so swiftly...as if she didn't want him to see it.

"It's a gift book," she said, her voice sounding strained. He began to focus on what was happening.

"It's a baby book for new mothers."

"My aunts are always having babies," she said. He became certain she wasn't telling him the truth. Suddenly, he felt as if he had walked into a moving truck. His head spun and his temperature shot up.

"Noah, are we going?" Biting her lip, she looked as if she were standing on hot coals.

Her warmth and showing him family pictures flashed through his mind. He jumped to a swift conclusion. "You're pregnant, aren't you?"

She didn't have to answer him. His heart skipped while he turned cold all over. He didn't think there was any other man in her life and hadn't been one for a long time. She was going to have his baby. "We used protection," he said, losing his usual habit of thinking before he spoke.

As she raised her chin, her face flushed. "A condom isn't a surefire guarantee."

"You're having my baby," he said.

"You always have been too perceptive," she said. Her eyes were bright and her cheeks red. "If I'd known you were coming into the building, I never would have left that book out. Pregnancy is something I can deal with, Noah. I know you're the father and we'll share responsibilities eventually, but don't rush me. I only just learned this myself."

"Can we talk about it?" he asked, his thoughts a jumble. For once, he couldn't rationally view a problem. That he was going to be a father kept running through his thoughts. Faith carried his baby.

A baby between them bound their lives together. At this point she couldn't cut him out of her life if she wanted to.

He drew her into his embrace. "We've got time to think things through. I'll admit, I'm shocked, but we'll work out what to do. How do you feel about it?"

"Once I got over the surprise, I reassured myself I have a big family who'll be supportive. This has been a shock to you. You'll have to give it time and thought, which is what I've been doing."

"You're right. I—" He was interrupted by her phone. When she answered, she began to talk business. In order to give her privacy he stepped into the hall. He was still lost in thought about his discovery.

The news of becoming a father was so unique, he didn't know how to deal with it. He'd given little thought to a family, always dismissing any contemplation of that as something that would occur in his distant future. Only now it had happened, so what should he do? He had to support his child and he wanted to support Faith if she would let him. He had never been one to duck responsibility and he wasn't going to on something that could be the most important event in his life.

He remembered his dad's words, "You'll find children are a blessing—they're important." For the first time, he saw how important he and Jeff had been in his workaholic father's life. A father who had always seemed totally obsessed about making money. With all his father's attempts to control his sons' lives, the attention, the focus on them, the influence—he and Jeff were as vital, or more so, to their dad as work. Why hadn't he ever seen this before?

Shaken again, Noah inhaled and tried to think straight. Strangely enough, he wanted to share the news with Jeff. It was too early for that.

First, he had to explore the new status with Faith.

Her door opened. "I'm off the phone. You could have stayed in my office."

"We were going to my house anyway. Let's go and we can talk more comfortably there."

"I'll get my purse," she said and disappeared inside.

As he drove, Noah had questions, only half listening when he asked her about her doctor visit. He still pored over the fact that he had gotten her pregnant.

The totally unexpected had happened. He had always been careful and cautious. He wondered about the future. Faith seemed to have dealt with the surprise and she didn't act as if she wanted to cut him out of her life. They had their families to consider.

"Noah, I can practically see the wheels turning in your head," she said.

"When you got the news, I'm sure wheels spun in yours. Of course, I'm mulling this over. It affects, me as well as you. Like it or not, we're in this together."

She became silent and he suspected she hadn't liked what he'd said. His dad would want him to marry her. *"You have enough wealth to do as you please and keep a woman happy. You'll find children are a blessing—they're important."*

Knox would consider this child particularly important. His first grandchild would give him instant access to the Cabrera business.

Noah glanced at Faith, suspecting she wasn't going to accept any hasty marriage proposal from him. It had taken time to get her back to bed for one night. A first in his life. Even so, of all the women he had known, in many ways, Faith was the one he would rather be involved with on a long-term basis.

She gazed out the window, lost in her own thoughts and he wondered what was the best course to follow. She wasn't happy. When would she have broken the news to him? He suspected more than a month from now.

With family problems between them, could they get along enough for him to propose to her? It was another question he had to tackle. He didn't have to propose if he chose not to.

"Care to share your thoughts?" he asked.

She gave him a level look. "I'm just thinking about practical matters. If I want to move in with Granddad or stay in my condo. My aunts will all want me. They are something to be reckoned with. I'm an only child, but my dad wasn't. He had four sisters and they have big families and they all live in this general vicinity. Our holidays are busy, homes filled to overflowing with kids and people. Weddings, funerals, babies—they're all big deals, particularly babies, because even the kids are interested then. Granddad is already a great-grandpa—six times, as a matter of fact. I have all sorts of family, so no being alone about this. Getting to be alone will be the deal. That was part of the charm in having a job away from Dallas for a while."

He smiled. "No such problem on my side of the family. At least the part about being alone. This will be my parents' first grandchild, Faith, so that's going to make this a big deal."

"I've asked Granddad and Angie to keep this quiet for a time, Noah. I want to think things through before all my aunts get wind of it. I'd appreciate the same consideration."

"Sure, I'll do the same with my dad. If you think *I'm* take-charge, you haven't ever dealt with my father." As she frowned, he suspected she would forever hold his last statement against his dad. "It's not so bad. He can't run your life."

"No, he can't," she said firmly, and he wondered if she was thinking about his dad or himself.

"One thing, Faith—and no argument over this. Don't even think about expenses. Let me pay them, whatever they are."

"Noah, you're already taking over," she said, sounding exasperated.

"Just agree, Faith. This is my baby, too, and part of my responsibility. You're not losing anything by letting me assume the cost. You get to deal with morning sickness. That's a fair trade-off."

She had to smile on that one and he felt a degree better. "I think I'd rather you'd take the morning sickness," she replied lightly. "I'd foot the expense to get rid of it."

"Sorry," he said, squeezing her hand.

"It's supposed to pass after the first three months. Why does three months sound like forever right now?"

"Until you get over morning sickness, can't you go in later to work?" he asked. "I can't imagine your grandfather objecting, and you'd get as much done."

"You're probably right," she admitted.

"We're going to become parents. That's an amazing realization," he said.

She continued to stare quietly at him. "I can't believe you are deeply interested. You're a bachelor and you've told me how you wanted your single life and your independence."

"I still want to be part of my child's life."

"We've got months to work out how we'll divide time, but that first year this baby needs to be with me."

"This is my baby, too, Faith. I want to be part of my child's life."

Her blue eyes flashed with fire even though she answered calmly. "I understand."

He felt the clash of wills. He wasn't giving up his child. There was no way he would let that happen. They had to work out something that would satisfy both of them.

Driving fast across the city, they soon entered a large exclusive area of mansions on acreages. She had known about the area, but never been in it before.

As they went through a gated area with a gatehouse and an attendant, she wondered at Noah's lifestyle. She had seen little of it except the yacht he rarely used. It was a five-minute drive from the gate before the mansion came into view.

"Now I understand some of the source of your self-confidence. Anyone who owns this would be supremely confident."

"There is a small note of contempt in your voice when you say that."

"No, not contempt. Don't you feel as if you're in a museum?"

He smiled. "Hardly. It's my home." Noah

drove around the Tudor mansion and stopped in back where more outbuildings stood with walls and trees hiding part of the view. A temporary solution came to him.

"Move in with me," he said. "I have a big house and you won't be alone. We can work our way through this."

Wide-eyed, she stared at him as if he had suggested they both move to the moon.

"What in the world? That makes no sense to me," she said, sounding sharper than before. "We're not in love, Noah. This was an accident, an unplanned baby. Well, now we have to plan, but there's no reason to move in with you. If I want to live with someone, I have relatives. I'm far closer to them than I am to you."

She was being stubborn and remote.

"Faith, I've told you I want to be closer to you and our baby." He didn't want to tell her that marriage was a quantum leap, but he wanted to do something to keep her where he could be involved in her life through this pregnancy. "I think it might be easier if we live together."

"Easier for you, perhaps."

"Easier for you. I'll get a nanny. I already have a full staff of people, a cook, a cleaning crew, a chauffeur. You would have some burdens lifted and could devote your full time to the baby," he said. "There's room for you and a baby, and we can easily stay out of each other's way."

"In this house, we could go a year and never see each other," she remarked.

"Think about living here," he said, growing impatient with her stubborn refusal to cooperate.

"I'll consider your offer," she answered quietly.

Fighting the urge to reach for her and pull her into his arms, Noah gave her a brief tour of his home. He grilled and later they sat on the patio to talk. All evening he had thought about their situation.

Maybe she needed time and space as much as he did. He'd had the solitary moments to think tonight while she had her phone call at the office, periods in the car on the drive back and right now to contemplate his future. The shock was easing slightly and thankfully, his mind was beginning to click. He kept mulling over her statement that the baby needed to be with her the first year. He had to agree even though he wanted his child in his life, too.

Finally, she said she had to get home.

"Faith," he said in a husky voice that stirred a tingle. She turned to him as he reached for her. "Nothing has changed about how much I want you." He pulled her into his embrace.

Her troubled blue eyes widened, their expression changing as her lips parted. "Noah," she whispered. He didn't know whether her whisper was protest or affirmation. All he knew was he wanted her. He drew her closer to kiss her. Her lips were soft and warm, opening floodgates of desire.

"You want this as badly as I do," he whispered, kissing her temple, her cheek, and then his mouth was on hers again. She wrapped her arms around his neck while he kissed her.

His hand drifted down her back and over her bottom, building desire that was already rampant.

She thrust her hips against him and he was on fire.

As he caressed her nape and trailed his hand lower to her buttons, she wriggled away.

"Noah, I need to stop and go home. The evening has been an emotional drain. I don't want to compound that by spending the night here."

He longed to draw her back into his arms, but he wanted to do as she wished. He ached to make love and to have her with him all night. Instead, he nodded, took her arm and headed back toward his car.

They were silent and he guessed she was wrapped up in her own thoughts. He hated to part. He wanted her with him, in his arms where he could make love to her. He didn't want to spend the next months this way. He suspected now, it would be more difficult than ever to get her into his bed. She was less than happy with him.

Whatever she truly thought or felt, he could only be certain about his own feelings. He wanted her with him. He wanted his child in his life equally as much.

As he drove her home, he thought about marriage. Sooner or later, his family would learn about the baby and then the pressure would be on to marry her. The fact that it was Faith made it easier to consider and far more appealing.

He got a cold knot in his stomach any time he thought about the permanency of commitment.

Yet the closer they drew to her house, the more he thought about kissing her again. The prospect alone aroused him. By the time they turned the corner for her condo, he was impatient to hold her in his arms.

He pulled into the drive and wanted to swear in frustration. Coming to meet them was Emilio Cabrera.

Her grandfather stopped in the yard and waited. The belligerent thrust of his jaw was as much an indication of his feelings as the fire in his eyes and the scowl on his face.

"Damn. I'm not going to get to kiss you good-bye," Noah said under his breath.

"Not this night," she replied. "I didn't know anything about this. Noah, Granddad is angry. I don't want him to talk to you until he cools down. Just let me out here and you go on your way."

"I'll do no such thing." As soon as they emerged from the car, Emilio turned to Faith.

"Faith, you go inside," Emilio said. "I want to talk to Noah."

"Granddad—" she started, but her grandfather waved his hand.

"Go inside. This conversation doesn't include you. If you stop me, I'll just go to Noah's office and that will be even less desirable for you, I'm sure."

"Granddad, you have high blood pressure. Let me deal with Noah. I'd just as soon you didn't interfere."

"You're sending my blood pressure higher. Soon we'll all be bound together by a baby, so you might as well let me talk to Noah now."

She clamped her mouth closed before turning

to Noah and shooting him a look that was far more threatening than her grandfather's. Noah wondered if he was going to get a beating by the old man. Whatever Emilio did, Noah would have to let him. He couldn't lay a hand on a man Emilio's age and he wouldn't think of hitting Faith's grandfather under any circumstances.

Faith went inside, closing the door, but Noah suspected she would watch the events unfold. He was certain Emilio would insist he propose to Faith.

"My granddaughter is carrying your baby."

"Yes, sir. I've asked her to move in with me and I've told her that I will take care of all expenses."

"That's good, but not good enough. Don't hurt her. Our families have never gotten along, but now we're going to have to. You keep her happy through this pregnancy."

"I'll do my best."

"If I were twenty years younger, you'd have a fight on your hands now, but I'm getting old and I know my limitations. There's no point in trying to fight you—it would be absurd. But you heed my words."

"I will, Mr. Cabrera. It's never been my intention to hurt Faith."

"I know your intention—it's to get control of the company."

"Not since I met Faith. I haven't been talking business to her. I gave up on that. My company will not try to buy yours."

"So now you're after Faith—only not for your wife," he said with anger lacing his voice. "I'm old-fashioned, getting out of touch with the world today, but in my family when a baby is involved, it means marriage. From my childhood, I've watched my grandfather and father fight Brands. I'm not overjoyed at the thought of a Brand marrying into our family, so maybe this is just as well."

"Sir, I'm trying to make my decisions about the future. I just learned that I'm going to be a father and Faith and I need to work out what we'll do."

Emilio waved his hand. "Go on with you. I've had my say." He turned away and Noah watched him walk to Faith's door, a door that opened instantly.

Noah waved to her and left, knowing there was no point in trying to talk to her with her grandfather in her house.

Eight

As soon as Noah had driven away, Faith faced her grandfather. "Granddad, let me take care of Noah."

"I just wanted a word with him. I didn't lay a hand on him. I didn't call him names or give him a lecture. I know you two have to deal with your future."

"Come in the kitchen and we'll get something to drink. Milk, juice—"

He shook his head. "I have to get home. I go to bed early."

"Let me drive you home," she said, getting her keys from her purse.

"It's still daylight. If I leave now, I'm fine." He placed his hand on hers as he shook his head. "Are you shutting Noah out? He has rights, Faith."

"I know he has rights. He can pay the expenses, do things like that. Now you get going or I'll worry. Unless you want to just stay here tonight. That's fine, too."

He smiled and hugged her lightly. "Nope. I'm on my way. I did what I wanted to do. When will you see him again?"

"Tomorrow night. I'm going to dinner with him."

"Fine. He said he's dropped trying to buy our business."

"Granddad, would you trust a shark or a tiger?"

He tilted his head as if thinking over his answer. "Nope, but it would behoove him to back off trying to buy us out at present. With a baby coming, he has sense enough to try to smooth relations between the families. Besides, he's smart enough to know if he proposes, he'll be far closer to having part of our company than ever."

"I'm not marrying Noah, Granddad."

"Don't hurt yourself and your baby because you're angry with Noah or because of business differences. You have a child to think about now. Your baby comes first."

"I know that," she replied solemnly, wishing she had never met Noah.

The morning passed in a blur. She couldn't concentrate on her work for thinking about Noah. There was no telling him goodbye permanently now. If only she could resist succumbing to his kisses. She hoped her grandfather didn't want to talk to Noah again. She didn't know if she would ever hear what had happened between them. She just prayed that he hadn't told Noah that he should marry her.

She couldn't imagine her grandfather or anybody else actually swaying Noah to do anything he didn't want to.

To her surprise, in the middle of the afternoon Noah called and asked if he could stop by the office and see her for a short time. Since it was a quiet afternoon she agreed, wondering what he had on his mind now.

When he breezed in, he looked as dynamic as ever.

"What brings this visit at three? I don't think you take off work often."

"I am today. Jeff called. He's here for a horse auction and before he goes back to the ranch, he wants me to sign some papers. He's in Fort Worth. I thought maybe I could persuade you to come with me and meet Jeff. It's a beautiful day. I want you to meet my charming brother and I'd like your company."

She smiled. "How can I resist that sales pitch? Actually, it's a quiet afternoon, so I'll go. You're your usual persuasive self, only you really didn't have to do any persuading."

"Great."

"I'll tell you now. You have to bring me back because I told Granddad I would spend the evening with him. He gets lonesome, Noah."

"So do I," Noah said, smiling. "But I'll give up the evening with you for your grandfather.

So, let's get going," he said, standing and waiting while she made arrangements to leave.

In minutes they were on the road. Noah had shed his suit jacket and his tie and she couldn't squash an undercurrent of excitement over being with him.

"How're you feeling today?" he asked.

"Fine since about eleven o'clock this morning. Maybe a little queasy every once in a while, but okay in general."

"Good news. Have you thought about moving to my house?"

"Of course. So far, that plan doesn't sound feasible, Noah. It would mean a far longer drive to work. I don't know what I'd gain from living at your house and you're seeing plenty of me now with the arrangement we already have."

"My powers of persuasion are slipping. I want you close and I think I could do a lot more for you and save you trouble. You won't have to cook or clean. You'll have my company," he said, glancing at her with a smile and she couldn't keep from smiling in return even though she was trying to shut out his arguments.

Moving in with him meant moving into his bed. With the fiery attraction between them she was certain that's what would happen.

"Jeff said he would meet us at his truck. He was still in the building and busy, but he thought he'd be through and outside by the time we arrive. If not, I told him we'd wait. It's a pretty spring day."

As they drove up to the arena and barns, she couldn't imagine Noah finding his brother easily. "Noah, this is a huge place."

"I've been here with Jeff and with Dad. I know where they park—in a shady spot, and if he's not outside, we'll go in. I can call him. There he is," Noah said and she spotted the twin brother.

"I see him, too. That's easy since he's your twin. So that's what you would look like as a cowboy." She smiled. "I can't imagine you liking the cowboy life."

"You're right. Jeff's got a renegade streak in him and I used to wonder if he did this just to annoy Dad, but Jeff truly loves it."

He slowed and stopped, walking around to

open her door as Jeff headed toward them and waved.

As he walked up, he greeted Noah while smiling at Faith.

"Faith, this is my brother, Jeff. Jeff, meet the best-looking Cabrera."

Jeff smiled as he turned to Faith and extended his hand. "It's nice to meet you. I've heard about you from my friend Millie."

"Just as I've heard about you from Millie and Noah."

"Your trailer is empty. Have you bought a horse?" Noah asked, wanting Jeff and Faith to get to know each other.

"Nope, I sold one," Jeff said easily, still looking at Faith. "No wonder my brother backed off trying to buy your company," Jeff said, amusement in his voice. "So you're the granddaughter I've heard about."

"Indeed I am," Faith replied with a smile. "And I intend to protect Granddad from all the Brands."

Jeff laughed. "I keep trying to convince her

that I've stopped all efforts to acquire Cabrera," Noah said.

"I can vouch for my brother," Jeff remarked, still smiling at Faith. "But then what I tell you probably doesn't carry any more weight with you than what Noah says."

"That's right," she replied.

"I'm delighted to meet you, Faith. You've got the best boots in the business. I can say this here to you, but not at my dad's house."

Faith laughed and Noah hated the jealous streak, a lifelong reaction, that pricked him, knowing that Jeff was simply being friendly and honest with her. Then he thought about Faith carrying his baby and his antagonism vanished. Jeff would become an uncle. While Noah wanted to tell Jeff, before he did, he wanted Faith's approval. Startled, he realized how much she had changed his life. When in his adult life would he have sought a woman's approval to do what he wanted? He knew he never had before, but now, with Faith, his life had changed. He looked at her as she chatted with Jeff and was astounded that he felt consumed by concern over her feelings and desires.

"I don't want to keep you two. Noah, let me grab the papers you need to sign from my truck."

He left them, quickly retrieving a manila envelope. He withdrew papers and a pen and handed them to Noah, who took them and placed them on the hood of his sports car.

"You two excuse me a minute and I'll take care of this," Noah said, turning away.

"I guess the old Brand-Cabrera family feud will be buried with you two," Jeff said with amusement in his expression.

"I think the feud is much more dominant in my family than yours. We have a strong sense of tradition. From what I get out of Noah, your family doesn't."

"No, and I don't know that I miss it. I guess if you've never known it, you won't miss it."

"If you're ever in our office, you might like to see my great-great grandfather's saddle. He made it for himself."

"Hey, that would be interesting. I think as far

SARA ORWIG 213

as use, I'll take the present day saddles. Much more comfy."

"I can't believe Noah's twin is a working cowboy. Noah doesn't seem to have one tiny bit of that in him."

"Not my mogul brother who loves the corporate deals. We're physically identical, they say, although we're not to each other. It ends there. We're different otherwise. You already know that."

Noah returned and handed Jeff the envelope with papers and pen inside. "That didn't take long."

"Thanks for driving out here. I'll be on my way and let you two go."

He turned to Faith. "And I'm really glad to meet you, Faith. Good luck with your career in the family business. That takes fortitude, but I imagine your family is far different from mine." Jeff stood. "See you soon, bro," he said, shaking hands again with Noah.

Noah watched Jeff climb into his truck as he held the car door for Faith. "I'm glad you met him. I wanted to tell him he will be an uncle, but I couldn't without talking to you about it first. If I ask him to keep it to himself, Jeff will."

"If that's the case, of course, go ahead and tell him. I was surprised—he doesn't seem exactly like you."

"I'm amazed you noticed in the short time he was here."

"When he first appeared, I thought you looked identical, but then after he talked to me a few minutes, I decided I can tell you apart even if you don't identify yourselves."

"You caught that quickly. Some people never do, and some do after knowing us a long time. Of course, the boots and jeans are a giveaway, but it's still easy for people who really know us to tell."

"I'm surprised you're so different."

"I can't explain why we are. I'm the one who feels the rivalry more than Jeff, I think." Noah confessed something that he had never admitted to anyone before.

She smiled at him. "I guess that's only natural with two competitive males. You shouldn't, though. You're highly successful and you each have different goals and likes in life, from what you've told me."

"Logically, I agree with you. Emotionally, when we get thrown into something together, I want to do the best. Actually, Dad has contributed to the rivalry. In many ways, all our lives he's pitted us against each other. When we get in something where there's competition, I want to beat Jeff."

"That's ridiculous, Noah, but I guess natural. He probably wants to beat you."

"Sure, he does. Then if something confronts both of us, we'll stick together."

"Sounds sort of like normal brothers, although I don't know what it would be like to have a sibling."

"You missed a lot. I can't imagine being alone and the only child all your life."

"It isn't bad at all and I don't know the difference."

"I wish I didn't have to take you back. I hope you saved tomorrow night for me," he said, glancing at her with a smile.

"Of course, Noah," she replied with amusement. "I took it for granted you'd want to see me."

"You can take it for granted," he said and his smile vanished. "I hope you've been thinking about moving in with me."

"I still don't see it at all. It would be far more inconvenient and complicated."

"We're not going to ruin a beautiful day with an argument. I'll work on another approach to this."

He turned to drive to the back door of the Cabrera building. "Thanks for going with me. I wanted you to meet Jeff."

"I'm glad you asked me. And it is a beautiful day. I'll see you tomorrow, Noah."

He leaned across the seat to kiss her lightly and then stepped out swiftly to come around and open the door for her.

"Until tomorrow," she said, going inside and hearing him drive away. Of course she was thinking about what he wanted her to do, but she wasn't moving to his house. Or into his bed. Yet she had been glad to meet Jeff who would be an uncle. The circle of people who knew about the baby was widening. It wouldn't be too long until everyone she dealt with found out.

She glanced around at the tree-shaded lot, wondering how her life was going to change in the coming year. And Noah's would change, too.

Dissatisfied over having to leave her, Noah returned to the office. While he sat at his desk, his thoughts were on Faith.

That night was the same. Sitting on his patio, he missed her, wanted her with him and knew he had to find a workable solution regarding her, the baby and their future.

He could marry her—it was the perfect solution if she was a woman he could live with forever. He didn't know if he'd ever be wildly in love, but he liked Faith more each time he was with her. She set him on fire; his desire was a constant, burning flame. He enjoyed being with her and thought she was a smart woman, trustworthy and reliable, all admirable qualities. Could he bear a permanent relationship? If he couldn't, he reminded himself that he could get out of it.

Faith, his baby, plus seven million from his dad into his account—why not? That would be the solution. The thought of Faith in his bed every night made him hot and he was certain his judgment would be warped if he thought about that aspect. He was duty-bound anyway.

The thought still gave him chills even when he knew it was the only course to follow. It was his duty. It was the wisest choice. She was a beautiful, desirable, intelligent woman, he reminded himself. Also, the seven million into his bank account was a plus. Good reasons to propose. That would settle so many arguments about what they would do in the coming year. Also, he missed her when she wasn't with him.

He sipped the beer he had opened before sundown. It was warm now, almost a full bottle. He barely noticed because he was lost in thought about a marriage proposal.

About ten he glanced again at his watch. She

would be home now because her grandfather went to bed early. Noah picked up his cell to call her.

Friday evening Faith strolled with Noah through his house to an informal living area. She was far more aware of his slight touch than her surroundings. The scent of his aftershave, his shoulder brushing hers, gave her a tingly awareness of him. Longing was intense, something she tried to ignore. If she lived here with him, she would be in his bed every night. Was she already in love with him in spite of all her logic and resistance and anger?

She glanced up at him and he looked at her. "What?"

"I'm just thinking about you living in this luxurious palace," she said, having no intention of revealing what she had been thinking.

So far he had stayed off talking about her moving to his house, and she had relaxed, enjoying the evening, knowing each hour spent with Noah added fuel to the attraction.

"Faith, am I going to get to think of names for this baby or am I out of that?"

"I'll be open to suggestions," she answered with amusement. He paused near a sofa and turned her to face him. One look in his gray eyes that held blatant desire and her insides fluttered.

"I missed you last night," he said in a husky voice. "I miss you whenever you're away from me." While he talked, he unfastened the clip in her hair, letting the locks tumble free over her shoulders.

Breathing was difficult and she looked at his mouth, longing to kiss him. He pulled her to him and his kiss shut out the world.

She became aware only of Noah's arms around her, his mouth covering hers, his lean, muscled body pressed against her.

"Noah," she whispered as he peeled away her dress. She ran her hands over him, unbuttoning and pulling his shirt free.

"I want you," he whispered between kisses as he walked her backward. She had no idea where he was leading her. Clothes fell aside as they walked and with each kiss, every step, she was more desperate for his loving. Her protests had vanished, forgotten now. She wanted him and wanted to make love to him.

"It's been forever," she whispered, not even aware she had said anything, wanting him desperately. Days and nights of longing had built need. Passion consumed her.

In minutes all clothes were gone and shortly he picked her up to carry her to a bedroom, coming down beside her on the bed to kiss and caress her. When he finally moved over her, kneeling between her legs, she caressed his hard thighs, relishing the sight of him before he lowered himself and entered her slowly.

She arched to meet him, wrapping her long legs around him and holding him tightly, soon moving with him until she crashed with her climax. He shuddered with his, pumping hard, sweat covering his brow and broad shoulders.

"Faith," he whispered and then came down, kissing her long and deeply. She held him close, relishing the moment and refusing to consider anything beyond this time with him.

He rolled onto his side, keeping her with him while he stroked her hair from her face. "You're beautiful and you set me on fire," he whispered.

"This is our moment, Noah. Right now. No tomorrows," she whispered, knowing that she had fallen in love with him and knowing just as well that the complications in their lives were still present, compounded by the baby.

"Faith, I want you in my life, both you and our baby," he said.

"Noah, enjoy the moment," she repeated. "I can't think beyond right now. I wasn't going to do this again and yet here I am. I don't want to think about our future."

While he showered light kisses on her temple and cheek, she stroked his shoulder and kept her mind a blank, concentrating on his marvelous body. Combing her fingers through his thick hair, she traced the contours of his ear and then ran her hand along his side and over his hip.

"I haven't slept nights. I think about you at work. You're in my thoughts constantly," he said as he continued caressing her.

She listened, her heart drumming with satisfaction over what he said. She was unwilling to admit to him that he had caused her sleepless nights, as well. She never wanted him to know how deep her desire ran.

When she finally mentioned showering, he stood and picked her up. "We'll shower together," he said, turning to carry her across a bedroom.

"Where are we?" she asked, looking at a luxurious bedroom with a king bed and fruitwood furniture, modern paintings on the walls that added color.

She lost interest, turning to look at him as she had her arms wrapped around his neck. His tousled black hair was damp around his face. His lashes were thick and amazingly long; his sexy eyes melted her protests every time he focused on her.

"We're in a downstairs bedroom. I wish I could just keep you here indefinitely."

"Don't be ridiculous," she said, smiling. "You'd tire of that fast enough."

"I think not. Let's try it and see who's right," he suggested with a twinkle in his eyes.

"You know better than that," she answered, feeling giddy and satisfied and excited all at the same time.

They showered and as before, desire rekindled and soon he picked her up to carry her back to bed and make love again.

Later they dressed, and Noah paused, turning to watch her. "You look beautiful," he said in a husky voice and her heart missed a beat as desire flared again.

"Noah—"

He held out his hand for her. "I want you more every day that goes by."

She stared at him. His gaze was intent again while he looked into her eyes and she grew more curious about what was on his mind.

He took her hand. "I've been mulling this over and I know you have, too. One thing we both want is this baby in our lives."

"You know I do."

"We get along, to put it mildly. We're going to

be parents. To me I know what seems the best solution for everyone."

"What's that?" she asked, steeling herself for whatever was to come.

"Faith, I want you. I want you to be my wife. Will you marry me?"

Nine

Her heart missed beats. Deep inside, she yearned to say yes, accept and see if he would fall in love someday.

"Noah! You don't mean that," she whispered.

"Of course I mean it. I've thought about it and about what I want to do."

Feeling light-headed, she closed her eyes momentarily and then she took a deep breath before looking at him again. "We're not in love."

"Given a chance, we can be. Dammit, Faith, you make it difficult when it doesn't have to be. I want you to be my wife. It's that simple," he said, frowning at her.

"When you first learned about the baby, you weren't overjoyed."

"I was shocked. Don't tell me your initial reaction wasn't surprise when you learned you were pregnant."

"Of course, I was surprised. But I'm happy about the baby."

"You're not thinking clearly about my proposal. If we marry, we could have so much, plus a family. I'm not after your family business. Can't you forget that was ever between us?"

"Hardly," she answered, unable to believe him. "Noah, your family wanted the business before you and I were born. That's gone on for generations."

"I can change that. What's important to me has altered. I've dropped trying to acquire Cabrera Leathers. I want to marry you."

"If it turned out that I got a message this week from my doctor that I'm actually not pregnant, would you still be pushing for marriage?"

"Faith, you're clearly pregnant, why speculate on it?" he said, sounding annoyed.

"I think I've made my point," she answered, hurting. He wouldn't propose if she wasn't having his baby. "You have a clear sense of duty, Noah, but that's not enough for me. I don't think that's what the foundation of marriage should be."

She pored over his proposal. No matter how she considered it, she came back to the same conclusion.

Noah would persist; she had already discovered his determination to get his way. Was she making life too difficult, as Noah said? His solemn expression mirrored her feelings. She had always imagined being in love with the man she married. Noah wanted her, but take away the sex and would there be anything between them?

At the same time, how easy it would be to accept. Let Noah go on his workaholic way and have her baby taken care of completely. If she accepted, at some point in time, Noah would take over Cabrera Leathers. She had no doubt of that outcome. Would he fall in love if they married? Part of her wanted to accept his proposal, but there was a cautious part of her that saw it as disaster.

He reached out to turn a lock of her hair in his fingers. "Think about my proposal. We can have a great marriage if you'll give us a chance. We'll give this baby two parents—and I can give our baby so much."

"And the fact that I'm part owner of Cabrera Custom Leathers makes no difference?" she asked.

"No. We'll have a prenup drawn up and you can put a clause in there that the Cabrera ownership you have will never go to your husband."

She nodded, deciding to talk to their attorney.

"Just think about it, darlin'. I want to marry you."

As she looked into his eyes, she could feel sparks between them, that electricity that kept desire simmering constantly. "You've had me in knots since I met you, Noah. I'll think about it."

"Good," he said, slipping his arm around her waist to kiss her until she stopped him.

"C'mon. If you won't stay the night I'll take you home."

"Noah, are you sure you aren't rushing into this? You've only known about the baby for a short time," she said as they walked through the house.

"Maybe, but I know this is what I want. It seems the best possible solution."

"Marriage shouldn't be the 'best possible solution'," she stated. That was one of the main reasons why she was reluctant to accept his proposal. "I have to give this a lot of consideration."

He walked her out to the car and held her door. He wasn't turning on the charm and she wondered if he was keeping quiet so she would have no distractions to take her thoughts away from his proposal.

His proposal and offer were incredibly tempting in too many ways. How easy it would be. She knew she already was strongly drawn to him. Live in that mansion and have Noah's help—her life would be transformed. She couldn't keep from thinking about it. It would be a more luxurious life for their baby. Her big family would love and help with her baby, luxurious extras didn't matter as much until the baby was older. Whether or not she moved in, she thought Noah would support his baby.

On the other hand, if she didn't accept his proposal, didn't move in—if he was sincere and truly drawn to her, he wouldn't drop out of her life.

At her door she kissed Noah until it was tempting to open the door and take him inside with her.

She finally pushed away. He held her hands. "Think about my proposal. It would be a good marriage, Faith. We already have so much between us. Let go some of those fears and reservations and take a chance with me."

"I'll think about it, Noah. It's a giant step, a commitment you didn't expect to take."

"A commitment I want now," he said, brushing her lips with a light kiss. "I want to be with you tomorrow."

She nodded. "I'll see you then," she said,

knowing he would call and they could make arrangements.

She paced her bedroom, keyed up, physically wanting Noah and wishing she could be in his arms this night. She always came back to the same thing—she didn't want a loveless marriage. The offer to move in with him was different. It wasn't as binding, not a true commitment, but that wasn't satisfactory, either.

If she had a full-blown intimate relationship with Noah, she would be better off to marry him and give her baby a real father. If she didn't marry Noah, would they have even greater struggles over Noah seeing his child? Was she going to have giant regrets?

She tried to use work to get through her morning sickness and push the Noah issue to the side. The queasy, uncomfortable feeling didn't pass as usual, but she continued working. At half past eleven she got a call from Millie, who was running errands and wanted to come see her briefly.

Something must be on Millie's mind, because

she had never come to the office. As soon as Millie was ushered into her office, Faith could see Millie's blue eyes were wide and filled with worry.

"You look as if you've had a disaster. What's happened?" Faith asked, bracing for bad news. "Is your family all right?"

"It's not me. It's you," Millie declared and Faith's curiosity grew. Their paths hadn't crossed often in the past year. Then she realized it had to be Noah. Had Millie heard something relating to the baby?

"What about me?"

"It's something I remembered. At first it didn't mean anything to me and I forgot about it. Now that you're seeing Noah more and you told me that he's proposed, it came to mind," she said. "When I saw Jeff and he bought those tickets from me, he'd been in town for his dad's birthday party."

"That must have been before I met Noah."

"I don't know. Jeff told me that at the party, he and Noah had a private talk with their dad, who made them an offer. Their folks want grandchildren," she said and dread filled Faith as she listened.

"Jeff's dad offered both sons five million dollars if they would marry within the year. Two million more to the son who marries first."

"Great. Just great." Faith clenched her fists. "An added incentive for him. The company he wants and seven million dollars on top."

"That might not be why he's proposed, but I thought you should know."

"Of course, I want to know. I wasn't going to accept anyway. Dammit, Millie, that's what he wants," she repeated, mulling it over with her anger growing. "I'm glad you remembered and told me. No wonder he's so persistent."

"Seven million is a fortune, but they already have fortunes made, so it may not have anything to do with Noah's proposal to you," Millie stated, a frown still creasing her brow.

"It has everything to do with his proposal, I'm certain. Noah calculates everything he does. Seven million is a fortune, even for Noah. He's not going to pass that by."

"Don't get all upset," Millie urged. She pushed

black strands of hair away from her face in a nervous gesture. "I hate to worry you."

"I'm not. It's just one more reason I don't want to marry him."

"You're not in love?"

"No, we're not," Faith snapped, angry, feeling her face flush, hurting and knowing that she *was* in love with Noah. "At least I won't be as attracted to him as before."

"I really don't know if I've done the right thing—" Millie said. "Are you going to be okay?"

"Yes, don't worry," Faith insisted emphatically. "You must have to get back to work."

Faith knew Millie was dedicated to her real estate job and had made a sacrifice to take time to come see her. "Thanks so much for telling me. I can't tell you how grateful I am that you did," she said, walking through the office to the front door with Millie. "Stop worrying. I would have found out sooner or later."

"You might not have," Millie said. "I told you because I would have wanted to know in your place."

With her anger building, Faith returned to her office and refused to take a noon call from Noah. Fury at him was hot, constant, keeping her from thinking about work. On top of that, she didn't feel well. She wanted to go home to bed, but she really wanted to have it out with Noah about the seven million from his father.

She had Angie take her home to get her car and she returned to the office.

Noah called and said he was coming to the office. She waited in her office. Everyone had gone except for Mr. Porter at his post as usual.

"Come in. I wanted to talk to you," she said as Noah neared. He followed her into the office and she closed the door. Windblown black locks of his hair fell over his forehead and he pushed his charcoal jacket open as he studied her.

"How're you feeling?" he asked, gazing intently at her. "You look pale."

"I don't feel well and I want to go home to bed, but we need to talk."

"Can't it wait if you don't feel all right?" he asked with a frown.

"No. We're alone here," she informed him. "I just discovered why you've proposed. Or at least one of the big reasons. You have several, I know. You want sex. You want your baby. You also want the seven million dollars from your dad, don't you?"

His expression didn't change and she realized he could hide surprise completely.

"I didn't propose to get seven million, I can promise you that. I have a fortune already."

"Come off it, Noah!" she replied. "Ambition oozes from your every pore. You are constantly trying to make more money."

"I swear I didn't propose to get that damn money my dad offered. I can't help what he does. Neither can Jeff. Where'd you hear about that?"

"That doesn't matter. You can go on your way," she declared through gritted teeth.

"Only part of you is angry with me. Part of you feels the same attraction I do. You won't let yourself trust me. I can't help what my father does, but I didn't propose to get his seven million."

"I'm sure it made proposing much more palatable and appealing."

"Of course it did. I'll admit that, but only on top of what I wanted to do anyway. If I hadn't wanted to marry you, the money wouldn't have mattered."

"I can't believe you."

He walked to her, placed his hands on her shoulders and held her, tilting her chin up to gaze into her eyes. His smoke-colored eyes had darkened and she didn't know whether it was from concern or anger. "I want you. I want to marry you. That has nothing to do with money or business. You should know me well enough by now to know that I'm more independent than that," he said.

Logic made her realize he was right, but she couldn't lose the notion that quickly because seven million was a fortune even if Noah didn't need to amass more.

"You're blowing this all out of proportion. The money would never cause me to propose. This isn't a good time to talk about it, Faith—you're not well," he said gently. "Let me take you to my house and I can take care of you tonight. And should we call your doctor?"

"No to both. I'm going home." She clutched her stomach and frowned.

"Then I'm taking you home," he declared in a tone that ended her argument. She was feeling worse by the minute and felt as if she had a discharge. She simply wanted to get home so she turned to get her purse. Suddenly she cramped, a sharp, severe pain.

"Noah..." she said, dropping her purse.

"That's it. We're calling your doctor. Sit down. What hospital do you go to?" he asked, striding around the desk to pick her up, letting her grab her purse. "See if you can be met at the emergency room."

She answered his question as she fished in her purse and retrieved her cell phone. In seconds, Noah sped toward her hospital.

As soon as she had talked briefly to her doctor about her symptoms, letting him know she was spotting and having cramps, she finished the call and glanced at Noah. "Dr. Hanover will meet me at the emergency room." She closed her eyes and put her head back again as cramps assailed her. She prayed she wouldn't lose her baby.

In what seemed forever even though she knew it was a short time, Noah arrived at the emergency door and parked, rushing around the car to lift her gently into his arms.

She was relieved she didn't have to walk inside and wrapped her arms around his neck.

"Hang on, darlin'. We're here."

"Noah, call Granddad. His number is in my phone. You take my purse, please. Tell him I just want him to know where I am and I'll call after I see the doctor. Don't make it sound alarming."

"Shh. I'll take care of it," Noah answered.

A nurse saw them and came running. To Faith's relief, she let Noah do the talking. The cramps, spotting and light-headedness frightened her and now she wished she had called earlier. She heard the nurse tell Noah where the waiting room was.

In minutes she was in a wheelchair and whisked away and the last she saw of Noah was him standing in the hall.

With his insides tied in knots, Noah went out to move his car. After he had parked, he called Emilio Cabrera to tell him Faith was in the emergency room and he would call as soon as the doctor came to tell him about Faith.

Noah's apprehension and worry grew by the minute. He didn't want Faith to lose their baby. She had looked frightened and worried when he left her and he hated having to wait helplessly, something so foreign in his life. Thankful he was the only person in the waiting room, he paced the floor. He hadn't been this frightened through his father's heart attack and surgery. He had worried about his dad, but he was alarmed now for Faith's well-being and their baby's survival.

Cabrera hurried in and crossed the room to shake hands with Noah. "Thanks for the call. You haven't heard anything yet, have you?"

"No, sir."

"We'll just have to wait. I wanted to come be with her when I can. Thanks for bringing her here."

"Sure." Both men were silent, Emilio sitting quietly while Noah walked to the window to gaze outside without seeing anything except how pale Faith had looked when he'd picked her up. He prayed silently, clenching his fist in his pocket, hating that he could do nothing to help her.

He didn't feel like talking to Emilio, and he suspected Emilio didn't feel like conversation, either. Time seemed to drag endlessly and finally Noah went back to sit by the older man.

"I'm surprised they are taking this long."

"Do you know when the doctor arrived?"

"No, I don't. I heard her place the call. Her doctor is named Farley Hanover. Do you know anything about him?"

"No. I just knew she had seen a doctor."

Noah made a mental note to check out Dr. Hanover. Dallas had fine doctors and medical centers and he wanted Faith to have the best.

He was glad she went to the same hospital his dad had been in for his surgery. "I know some of the doctors with this hospital because this is where my family goes, but I don't know obstetricians," he said.

"My doctor is with this hospital, so I guess that's why she's stayed with it. She grew up with family doctors and her pediatrician is connected here."

They lapsed into silence again and Noah was uncustomarily prickly, nervous and on edge, something he'd never before experienced. After a few moments, he had to stand and move around.

A doctor appeared at the door and entered the room. "Mr. Cabrera? Mr. Brand?"

As they stood, he joined them. "I'm Farley Hanover. We're checking Faith. Her vital signs are good. We've given her something and we're doing some tests now. When we're through tonight, we'll move her to a room. She needs to stay off her feet and we want her here tomorrow for further tests. As soon as we move her, we'll let you know and you both can go see her."

"Thank you," Noah said at the same time Emilio did. "What about the baby?" Noah asked.

"We'll know more soon," Dr. Hanover said and left them.

"More waiting," Noah said, thankful he'd gotten Faith to the hospital, but wishing she had called her doctor earlier in the afternoon. "She didn't feel well at breakfast, but it wasn't dire and I figured it was her usual morning sickness. So did she."

"I'm glad you got her here. I suspect she wouldn't have been here as soon if she'd been on her own."

They were silent again and to Noah the hours seemed to drag more than ever. "Mr. Cabrera, I'm going to the gift shop and see if I can get her some flowers."

Emilio stood. "If you don't mind, I'll join you and get her something."

They went to the gift shop near the hospital entrance and in minutes Noah had a bouquet

of roses ordered for her room. He found a
robe and bought it and slippers to match while
Emilio selected a mixed bouquet and a book.
Noah picked up a brightly colored bag that held
a comb and brush and toothbrush and paste.
Her grandfather added a bottle of perfume and
lotion. They waited for the gifts to be wrapped
and took with them back to the waiting room.
It was after nine when they were finally sum-
moned by a nurse and given a room number.

As they rode in the elevator, Noah turned to
Emilio. "Sir, I'd like to stay with her tonight
unless you intend to."

"If you're staying, I'll go home. I hope
she's well enough she doesn't need anyone all
night."

"Even if she is, I'd like to stay in case she
wants anything."

Emilio nodded. "That's good."

When they reached her room, Noah held
the door for Emilio and followed him inside.
With most of her long hair falling across her
shoulders, Faith was lying in bed. Aching for
her to be well again and the baby to be all

right, Noah longed to take her in his arms and hold her, but he knew he couldn't. Instead, he watched Emilio kiss her cheek and hold her hand.

"I'm glad you're here. I came when Noah called."

"You didn't need to—I'll worry about you driving home."

"I'll make it home," he said, turning to Noah. "Here's Noah."

Emilio moved away to pull a chair close by her bed while Noah went to the other side of the bed to take her hand. "Are you feeling any better?"

"Yes, I am. Thanks for getting me here and thanks for the beautiful roses." She turned to Emilio. "Granddad, thank you for your flowers. You know I like them."

"I brought you something," Noah said, placing his gift on the bed beside her. "So did Emilio."

Her grandfather placed his gift on the other side of the bed.

"Thank you both," she said, picking up

Emilio's present to unwrap her book and thank him.

Next she unwrapped Noah's. "Thank you," she said, smiling faintly. "Looks like you thought of everything."

"Your grandfather selected the perfume and lotion," Noah said.

She touched the robe and slippers. "I'll wear these tomorrow. That's great. Thank you both. I was wondering how I could get my robe here. Now I won't have to."

"Sure," he said, sitting quietly and letting Emilio talk to her. "If you two would like to be alone," Noah offered after a few minutes, "I can step into the hall."

She glanced at her grandfather, who shook his head. "I don't think so, unless there's something you want," he told her.

"No, Noah, please stay. It was nice of you to offer," she answered. To his relief her color looked normal, with her cheeks rosy. But her voice sounded tired and he suspected they had given her something for sleep. An IV dripped slowly. Tomorrow he wanted to talk to the doctor again, but he hoped he could do so after they had finished all their tests.

In a short time Emilio stood. "I'll be going now. If you want anything, call me and I'll come see you in the morning."

She squeezed his hand. "Please call me, Granddad, after you get home."

He nodded, kissed her cheek again and patted her hand. "'Night, Noah," he said, picking up his cap and heading out.

Noah moved close to the bed to take her hand. "I wish I could do something. I hate this."

"There isn't anything. Thanks for all you have done tonight."

"You look sleepy. Go on, sleep. I'll take the call from your Granddad."

She nodded and closed her eyes. In minutes, Noah knew she was asleep. A chair in the corner was a recliner. He moved the phone near it and got out her cell phone in case her grandfather called on that. Kicking off his shoes, shedding his coat and tie, he stretched out, putting his feet up, still praying that she would be all right and their baby was safe.

Soon the cell phone rang and Noah answered instantly, glad to see it hadn't disturbed Faith. "Sir, she's sleeping," he told Emilio quietly and her grandfather finished the call quickly.

Noah settled back to wait, wondering what had caused her trouble and hoping it wasn't serious. He thought about their fuss over the money he would get if he married and how upset she had been. The money was of such small importance and he hoped she forgot all about it for now.

Faith stirred and looked around. The windows were gray with early-morning light. Startled, she spotted Noah stretched out in a recliner. He opened his eyes and met her gaze.

"What are you doing here?" she asked, surprised that he would stay. "You didn't need to stay with me."

"This is where I wanted to be," he said, sitting up and swinging his feet off the recliner. He was rumpled, his hair tousled, just as she imagined hers was. "How do you feel now?"

"Better," she said. "You shouldn't have stayed, Noah."

He shook his head. "If I'd been home, I would have worried more. Emilio called as soon as he got home, which was rather soon. He'll be here today."

"I fell asleep. I intended to stay awake until Granddad's call, but I couldn't. Now you go on, because I know you're busy."

"I'll leave for a short time and be back in a few minutes. I want to see the doctor," he said, standing.

Her throat knotted over all his attention and care. His solicitousness threatened to defuse the anger she had been feeling toward him. He had been only kind and caring since yesterday afternoon. She didn't want to be more in love with him, but his attentive manner was making it difficult for her.

"I want you to be okay," he said. His voice was deep and thick, and she was surprised how caring he sounded. "You and the baby."

"I know, Noah. I do, too," she whispered.

"I don't want to leave you for a moment,

but I'll be right back," he said, stepping into the quiet hall and pulling the door closed behind him.

She sighed, knowing his kindness drew her to him more than ever.

In minutes he returned with his hair combed. He looked virile, healthy and strong. She couldn't keep from being glad he was with her.

The nurse appeared and Noah stepped out into the hall to give them room, returning as soon as she left.

"You might as well go on your way for now. I've already called Granddad and told him not to come until I call him back. They have tests they intend to do right away and you won't be able to see me anyway. I think I'll be busy for quite a while, but I don't really know. I hope they release me sometime this morning."

"I may run an errand, go downstairs and eat, and then hang around. I'd like to see your doctor."

She smiled at him. "I'll tell you what he says. Go on, Noah."

"I'll be back." He crossed to the bed to give her another light hug and kiss before he left. She watched him walk out and close the door behind him, feeling another pang.

The morning was as busy as she had expected. When she was wheeled back to her room, Noah and her grandfather both arrived.

They stayed while she was brought lunch. Finally, her doctor came and Noah and Emilio once again stepped into the hall.

It was too long a wait for Noah, who wondered what was happening when finally the door opened and Dr. Hanover walked over to them.

"Faith can tell you, but she also said you'd want to talk to me. She said I could tell you that she is going to have to stay off her feet for the rest of this trimester. Hopefully, after that she will be better and can get up again, but her activities will be restricted even then."

"What about the baby?"

"Everything should be fine if she takes care of herself and does as she should. She said she lives alone, but has a big family who will help. For this first trimester she really shouldn't be alone because she must be absolutely off her feet except a few steps to the bathroom."

"I'll move her in with me if she'll let me. She won't be alone ever. I have a full staff and can hire a nurse," Noah said, determined that's what he would do.

"You won't need a nurse if Faith will cooperate. She can give you more details," her doctor said.

"Thanks, Dr. Hanover," Noah replied.

Emilio thanked him, as well, and turned to Noah. "She can stay at my house if she wants, but you'd be able to do more than I could."

"I'd really like to take care of her, sir," Noah said, wishing Emilio would advise Faith to accept help.

Emilio nodded. "If you'll wait a moment, I'll talk to her about it."

"Thanks," Noah said, hoping she'd listen to both of them as he watched Emilio disappear into her room. He paced the hall while Emilio was gone far longer than Noah expected. He wondered what was happening and whether she would agree to stay at his house.

Finally Emilio stepped into the hall. "You talk to her. I think she'll stay at your house."

"I want her to. I don't want to upset her, either," Noah said, worried and feeling frustrated because he was still running into events over which he had little control.

"I'll wait out here and you let me know. If she won't go to your house, then I'm going to insist she come to mine."

Noah nodded and took a deep breath, going in to talk to Faith. Her blue eyes were clouded by distress and he knew she was unhappy over the doctor's diagnosis.

"Sorry, darlin'," he said, pulling a chair close and sitting beside her bed. "Just remember this is temporary."

"I can't be on my feet. I can't go to the office. Granddad doesn't want me to work at home at all."

"He's right. You need to relax and rest, take care of yourself and our baby."

She focused on Noah and clamped her lips

together. She looked on the verge of tears and his concern increased. "Darlin', come home with me and let me take care of you. I talked to Dr. Hanover about it and he thought that was a good plan. Your granddad is older and you don't want to pull both of you out of the business."

She bit her lip and frowned. Noah hated to worry her more about her grandfather, but he thought that was the only reason that might convince her to let him care for her.

"You're right, of course. I don't want to take him away from the shop," she said. She looked at Noah intently. "Noah, tell me truthfully, are you making this offer because you feel you should?"

"I promise, I'm not. I could offer to send help to your house or your grandfather's, but I want you at my house, darlin'. I really mean it." He hated to point out to her the alternatives, because she probably would prefer them, but he did want her at his home and he was surprised at how much. "I have plenty of rooms if your aunts and cousins and grandfather and whoever else want to stay at my house part of the time with you."

She gave him a faint smile. "You have no idea what you're offering." Her smile disappeared and the anxiety returned to her expression. He waited, giving her time to think it over.

"All right, Noah," she sighed. "I don't mean to sound ungrateful. It's just that I never planned on getting sick and it's hard to give up my autonomy."

"Just keep remembering this is temporary."

"I keep telling myself that, although it could be longer than the first trimester, but that's what they expect."

"The time will pass, I promise you. Probably sooner than you think. Dr. Hanover said he'll release you when you know where you'll go and who will take care of you. Your grandfather is waiting in the hall."

"You can go tell Granddad and then let Dr. Hanover know, please. The care is good, but I'd rather be out of the hospital."

Noah bent down to slip his arms around her again and kiss her lightly. "Don't worry. You can have whatever you want. You'll have to do what your doctor says, but other than that, I'll do anything."

She hugged him. "I hope you mean what you say about really wanting me to move in."

"I do. I told you and I meant it." He released her and straightened to see her wipe her eyes. "Stop worrying, Faith," he said. "That doesn't help our baby."

She smiled at him. "Thanks, Noah," she said.

He left to get her grandfather and then went to find the doctor to see about her release. He intended to get an ambulance to take her to his house. Thank heavens she had agreed to go home with him. He was constantly amazed by the turn of events in his life since he met Faith. He never thought he'd feel so strongly about a woman, particularly one he had not been involved with in a serious relationship. With Faith in his house where they could be together for the months to come, surely she would accept his proposal. His pulse quickened at the prospect.

Ten

"Noah told me you'll stay at his house." Emilio came to sit beside her bed. "Are you doing what you want to do?"

"Yes, Granddad. Noah will have all kinds of help for me. You can even come stay at his house if you want."

Emilio nodded solemnly. "I'm glad. I just want you to take care of yourself and not worry about business."

"I won't," she promised, patting his hand. He held her hand.

"Sorry, honey. I hate for this to happen to you."

"At least there's something I can do. They say the baby should be fine."

"That's what's important. You hold to that."

"I will have a long list of things I need from my house. Can Aunt Stephanie and Aunt Sophia get everything for me and bring it to Noah's when I get moved?"

"Of course they will." He grinned. "You know your aunts. They'll be overjoyed to help you and equally thrilled at the prospect of getting to look at Noah's house. I didn't tell them you're here because they'll all descend on you." His smile faded and he studied her while he patted her hand.

"What is it?" she asked. "You look worried."

"Honey, I had last night to think about this. At this point, I need your approval. Under the circumstances, I'd like to sell the business to Noah—"

"Sell? No." She tried to sit up, grimaced and fell back on the pillows.

"Faith, I shouldn't have told you, but I have to. I don't want to worry you, honey. You know that. I've given this thought, and I'll tell you why."

"Granddad, don't do that," she said, shocked by his decision and hurt because she knew she was the cause.

"Now listen to me carefully. If I sell to Noah, I would receive an income to retire on comfortably. Noah will pay an exorbitant sum—he's already offered one. It'll give us money for the baby now, which will be good. Business is slipping each year. Why wait until it's worse and we don't get as much?"

"Granddad, until last night you didn't want to sell. You told me you wanted to work at least ten more years if your health is all right. How can you turn your back on the work you love? Noah will take care of my expenses and the baby's later. I don't want you to sell." She had a panicky feeling that everything around her was slipping out of control.

"I'm still thinking it over, Faith. All of us working on the leather now are older and frankly, I don't think we can be easily replaced.

If I want to work, I can always find work and demand the hours I want."

"That's true, but it's not the same as working for your own company. A company that's been in the family for generations," she said, trying to stay reasonable.

"Change is inevitable and you know it."

"So many changes all at once. I think you're rushing into this. Take several months to think it over."

He nodded. "I will, but at the same time, I want you to give it consideration. This looks like the best possible thing to do and right now, we could get a huge sum of money from Noah. I don't want to wait until he changes his mind."

Relieved at the possible reprieve, she hoped that was the last she would hear about it.

"I'm going to the office. Noah gave me his phone number and I'll come see you tonight once he has you settled." She smiled as he leaned down to kiss her cheek. "Do what you're supposed to."

"I will. I promise," she replied, wondering

what it would be like to live under the same roof with Noah for months.

It took far longer for her to get out of the hospital than she had expected. By midafternoon Noah had arranged for her to be transferred to his house by private ambulance. Soon she was ensconced in one of the bedrooms in the east wing.

He introduced her to staff who would help, and finally everyone else vanished and she was left with Noah. He had changed to khakis, a knit shirt and loafers and he looked energetic, healthy, always appealing.

Sitting on the edge of her bed, he held her hand. "I'm glad you're here. A nurse is coming tomorrow to help you get up the little you're allowed to."

"Thank you," she said, amazed by all he was doing for her.

He caressed her throat lightly. "I want you well and happy. Think about marriage, Faith. It would be good if we married now."

"Noah, I can't get out of bed, much less to a wedding."

"I can marry you right here and we'll have a big ceremony later. That's not a problem."

She gazed at him solemnly. "You've been good to me during this. I'll think about it." She turned to kiss him deeply and he returned her kiss with heat. For the first time she felt better about the prospect of marrying him. He couldn't possibly be more caring right now. Yet she dared not hope for love because it would be crushing later to realize it was only his corporate practicality speaking.

Looking around, she already felt better just being out of the hospital. Noah had done everything possible for her. She looked around at her luxurious surroundings, the pale yellow bedroom with splashes of white and green, so elegant after the hospital. She thought about Noah and admitted to herself that she was in love with him. Deeply, probably forever. What did he really feel toward her, she wondered? The seven million from his father couldn't be overlooked. It was a huge incentive to marry.

Questions buzzed in her thoughts and she knew she shouldn't worry or get upset over their future because it wouldn't help her health to be stressed. In any other situation Noah's proposal should have been the most joyous occasion.

Her grandfather called to see if she was comfortable and she told him once again that she didn't want him to sell the business.

"Faith, think about the future. Noah may be there for you and he may not. You've had a rocky time with him."

"That's past now," she said, hoping it was and wondering if there would be more major disagreements.

"I'll do whatever I think is best," he said, leaving her worried because he wouldn't promise to avoid selling.

That evening Noah carried her to the patio to eat. He picked her up to place her on a chaise and then gave her a tray with her dinner.

"Noah, this is delightful," she said, thankful to be outside and out of the hospital.

"Someone will come to the house to do your hair."

She shook her head. "I've complicated your life and mine."

He took her hand and brushed her knuckles with light kisses. "I think we complicated our lives. It wasn't you alone."

For the next three weeks she began to feel better, but knew she had to do as the doctor said and rest. When her grandfather came to see her and brought her a bouquet of lilies, daisies and roses, he sat beside her bed to chat.

"Faith, I wondered whether Noah told you. I asked him to wait until we had a deal. He's bought the business."

"Granddad!" she cried, her tranquility shattering. "No! You said you'd think it over."

He held up his hand. "I thought it over carefully. I promise, I did what I wanted to do. And don't get all upset over this because it won't be good for you. I can retire and travel. I can enjoy life and take it easy."

"That doesn't sound at all like you," she said. "You didn't tell me."

"No, I didn't want to worry you."

"You don't think *this* won't worry me? Noah bought your company?"

"Yes," Emilio replied. "Faith, I got a marvelous price—three million dollars. We have a small leather company. It doesn't come close to being worth three million. I'll set up a trust for the baby. You own part of the company, so you are going to get a lot of money, too."

"Granddad, if this hadn't happened to me, you would never have sold," she said, fighting tears.

"Perhaps not, but it did happen and things change. I'll repeat and you listen—I did exactly what I wanted to do."

"You did what you *thought* you should do."

"It's done—so accept it. Stop fretting and think about what we have now. Honey, the sale is generous, so very good. We could never get that much money for the business anywhere else. Noah wanted it that badly. It's an exorbitant price. On the regular market, it would have gone for half a million tops, I'm sure."

"Granddad, that still doesn't make selling a good thing to do," she said, frustrated, angry and hurting for her grandfather. "Does the family know?"

"Everyone is delighted, because they all own small parts and they will get money, too."

Looking down, she knotted her fists. She knew she wasn't making her grandfather happy, but all she could feel was anger toward Noah. She wanted out of his house and away from him.

When her grandfather left her to her thoughts, she wanted to cry. Noah had gotten what he wanted. All because of her doing.

She reached for her cell to call information for the number of a private ambulance company. She could afford to move back to her grandfather's and now it wouldn't interfere with him and his work.

When he returned to the office on his first day back, Noah looked at Holly, really looked at her, because her customary friendliness had vanished. For the first time he noticed that her engagement ring had disappeared and her coloring was pale.

"Holly, are you all right?" Noah asked.

She raised her head and her green eyes flashed

with fire. "Not exactly. You don't look so great yourself."

"I'm worried about Faith. She blames herself for the sale," he said, more to himself than Holly.

"Mr. Cabrera called you about the deal."

"Faith thinks he wouldn't have done that if it hadn't been for her difficulties."

"He probably wouldn't have. Sorry, because you've finally gotten what you wanted. As far as my life, I've broken my engagement. Actually, he broke it and moved my stuff out of our apartment."

"Damnation. Sorry to hear that," Noah said, momentarily forgetting his own troubles, feeling gloomier because his secretary was in a slump.

"Better now than later," she said, gathering papers and leaving the room.

Noah stared after her, thinking about his own problems. He had what he had wanted badly, but he didn't feel happier or more satisfied. His father was jubilant over the purchase of Emilio's business, but Noah experienced a growing sense of loss.

Faith wanted him out of her life. He was unhappy, frustrated, at a loss.

Acquiring Cabrera Custom Leathers was insignificant next to his relationship with Faith. He didn't give a damn about the leather business if it meant tearing them apart. That realization shook him. Nothing else mattered as much as Faith. Noah raked his fingers through his hair. He was in love with her. He didn't even know when he had actually fallen in love with her, but he loved her and she was vital to his life. Why hadn't he recognized the depth of his feelings for her? He'd been so blinded by desire.

He jammed his hands into his pockets and rocked back on his heels. He wanted her more than he wanted the Cabrera business. Of course, if he canceled the sale, the old man would be unhappy with him. Then she wouldn't be happy, either. He sincerely thought her grandfather was jubilant over the money he was getting. Mr. Cabrera had already told Noah he would work for him on a contract basis.

Noah figured that still wouldn't be enough to please Faith. He paced his office, mulling over possibilities of what he could do to get her back. Finally, he picked up the phone to place a call to Emilio Cabrera.

Eleven

Faith was propped in bed. Noah had called and set a time to see her. At the thought of letting him back in her life she always came to the same conclusion. She wanted her grandfather to be active, healthy and happy. Noah had taken that away from him.

The seven million from Noah's dad rankled, although if that had been the only dispute between them, she could have accepted it—it would be a paper marriage anyway. And there would have been hope that love would develop.

She was the one who had sent Noah packing—

she suspected it hadn't sat well with him, and he wanted to try to cajole her into changing her mind. If he had tired of her he wouldn't have taken the task. This was probably a useless visit on his part, but he had asked politely and she had consented to a short visit.

Promptly at five o'clock Noah appeared in the doorway. He must have come straight from work because he was still in his suit. The sight of him still was a thrill in spite of her anger.

"You look great. I hear bed rest is going okay."

She nodded, watching him cross the room. He shed his jacket and tie and her heart beat faster, remembering times he had done the same before making love to her. She wanted him desperately in spite of her simmering resentment. At the same time, his determination to always get what he wanted created an unbridgeable gap.

Sitting beside her on the bed, he took her hand as he leaned down to brush her lips with a kiss.

"Noah," she started to protest. If only she

could wrap her arms around his neck and pull him close.

Holding her hand, he rubbed her knuckles lightly. His eyes were warm, filled with desire that fanned the flames she felt. Nothing he did could stop her from wanting him, no matter what trouble lay between them.

"I've talked to your grandfather," Noah said, surprising her. "I've made him another offer and he's accepted."

Shocked, she drew a sharp breath. "What? What are the two of you doing behind my back now?" she blurted. "Granddad hasn't called."

"No. I asked him to wait and let me talk to you first. He'll call."

"This again," she said, frowning. "The two of you deciding who will talk to me and break the next bit of news over something no one has asked my opinion about." Her curiosity climbed and she stared at Noah, hoping it wasn't more bad news, wondering what he had done. "What was your offer?"

"I'll put the company back in his owner-ship if he will agree to letting Brand handle

Cabrera leather products exclusively. He will be under contract to Cabrera and I'll pay him three million for this deal. Thereafter, he will get thirty percent of the profits each year, plus salaries and benefits from Brand. If he ever decides to sell the company, we have exclusive rights to buy. We turn him down, he's free to go elsewhere."

"Oh, Noah!" she cried. She had a knot in her throat as joy flooded her. "Thank you! I'm so happy you made Granddad that offer. It's perfect." Noah's generous act wiped the slate clean. Her grandfather could go back to the work he loved. She raised her head to kiss Noah. Instantly, his arm went around her waist and his tongue thrust into her mouth. He held her tightly, bending down to lean her back against the pillows while he kissed her passionately. Desire was white-hot, yet she reined it in, trying to bank her longing and need.

"Noah, I'm so happy." She gazed up at him jubilantly. "That's the most wonderful news."

"Emilio seems pleased, too," Noah said, brushing her hair away from her face lightly.

"You're beautiful, Faith. I've missed you like hell."

She squeezed his hands. "Thank you. You did this for me."

"I sure as hell did. We'll do well with this—everyone is pleased." He framed her face. "Faith, I've missed you."

Faith's heart thudded as her happiness increased. "I've felt the same."

"I talked to my dad and told him you wouldn't marry me because of that stupid cash offer."

"Oh, Noah!" Implications of what he was saying bombarded her. "You really do care."

"Of course, I care. I love you, Faith."

She gasped with surprise and gladness, throwing her arms tightly around his neck again to pull him to her to kiss him.

Finally, she pushed away. "You've never told me. I had no idea—"

"I haven't acted like a man in love?" he asked drily.

She laughed, feeling giddy with happiness. "Maybe so, but it's heaven to hear you declare it. I love you and I thought I'd never hear you say the same. I'm the happiest woman on earth."

He pulled a small box out of his pocket and placed it in her hand. "For you," he said. "Will you marry me?"

Holding the box, she looked up at him. "Yes! Yes, I'll marry you." She kissed him again joyfully.

"My dad is as stubborn as they come. He said he wasn't giving up on letting me have the seven million because he made a deal with us, but what he will do is put the money in a trust fund for our baby."

"Noah, that's wonderful. You know I don't care about the money. I've missed you so. My life has been dull and lonely and miserable without you."

He kissed her. Once again she stopped him, knowing each time grew more heated and passionate, more intense, and they weren't going to be able to take it further.

"Hey, careful. Don't hurt yourself," he said.

Smiling at him, she picked up the ring box to open it and see a smaller black box. A deep breath escaped her as she saw the dazzling large diamond surrounded with diamonds and sapphires nestled inside.

"Noah, this is the most beautiful ring in the world," she said. He took it from her to slip it on her finger.

"I love you, Faith, and I want you to be my wife."

"I love you. You'll never know how much," she said, laughing with joy. Her smile faded. "I don't know if the doctor will allow a wedding."

"Why not? We can get married right here in this room with just our families. Then after the baby comes, we can have the big wedding or just a big party."

"You're already thought that out." Amusement colored her words.

"I'll admit I have. I didn't intend to let you turn me down."

"A small wedding will be grand. Thank goodness this is a huge suite! My aunts and cousins will fill it. Later, I think I'd like the whole wedding ceremony. I've always dreamed about my wedding dress."

"Whatever you want suits me fine," he answered, smiling at her.

"If we have a healthy baby my happiness will be complete. You're right. The old family feud isn't so important," she said, returning to studying her ring.

Smiling, she looked up at him and wound her arms around his neck to pull him closer. "This is wonderful. I'm thrilled, Noah. I love you without bounds."

Epilogue

Faith barely noticed the packed Dallas church, because all she could see was Noah waiting at the end of the aisle. Her aunt Sophia held their five-month-old baby, Emily, and all her family was present. Millie, as maid of honor, stood waiting with Faith's bridesmaids—two friends and four cousins.

Faith linked her arm with her grandfather's and glanced at him. "Ready?"

"I'm happy for you, honey. Noah is a good man and you have a beautiful baby. I hope you have all the happiness your grandmother and I had."

She kissed his cheek lightly as the wedding planner said, "Faith, it's time."

Her gaze returned to Noah, who stood, watching her, as she walked on her grandfather's arm. As she passed her aunt Sophia, she glanced at Emily, who slept peacefully, and Faith's joy grew. Emily was a beautiful baby with Noah's black hair and her blue eyes.

Before she knew it, Emilio had placed her hand in Noah's and sat in the pew by her aunt. Noah held her hand, smiling at her, and her heart raced with eagerness.

She had returned the plain gold wedding band for this occasion and after repeating their vows again, Noah slipped it onto her finger beside her sparkling diamond-and-sapphire engagement ring.

Noah kissed her, his mouth warm, inviting, too briefly on hers, and then they were introduced to the guests as Mr. and Mrs. Noah Brand.

She floated up the aisle and into the lobby on Noah's arm and he turned to her.

"I can't wait for us to be alone."

* * *

Noah couldn't ever recall being as happy as he had been since marrying Faith. Today was the best of all. They would take the honeymoon they hadn't been able to have before and he tried to keep his thoughts in the moment, though he was already anxious to go.

While Faith posed with her attendants, he stood aside, watching. He had married the most beautiful woman he had ever known. Her strapless white dress fitted closely with a straight skirt and an attached train. It revealed her lush curves and tiny waist, her figure that had returned to pre-pregnancy size. It amazed him how quickly and completely she had her figure back after giving birth to Emily.

He felt blessed to have Faith and Emily in his life.

They finally departed for the country club where he had won the bid at the fateful auction, which seemed so long ago. Yet not until the first dance did he finally have Faith in his arms.

"This day is aeons long," he remarked. "What

gets me through it is the sight of you and the thought of later."

She laughed. "It's a day I'll always remember. Thankfully Emily is being her usual placid self."

"Her personality is definitely from your side," he replied, meaning every word. That they had a serene, peaceful baby constantly surprised him, even after six months.

"I quite agree," Faith answered blithely as he groaned. "Oh, oh. Here comes Jeff to dance with you."

When his brother approached, Noah said, "I was just telling her that here comes my pesky twin to take her away from me for a dance."

"How right you are. May I?" he asked, turning to Faith.

"Not on your life," Noah interrupted.

Laughing, Jeff turned and walked away.

Noah grabbed her and kissed her passionately until she leaned away slightly to look up at him. "Noah, I'm as happy as it's possible to be. You've given me the world by marrying me, by giving me Emily, by allowing Granddad to keep his business."

"You've given me more happiness than I've ever known. You and Emily."

"Darlin', when we get alone tonight, we're staying right there. You had your chance. Southern France later. Honeymoon delights now. I'm so in love with you I can't think straight or concentrate on anything else," he answered solemnly, leaning down to kiss her again.

She raised her mouth to his, overjoyed and filled with love for her tall, handsome husband who had changed her life forever.

* * * * *